W9-BYD-771

. . .

BAILEY'S
WINDOW

HARCOURT BRACE JOVANOVICH, PUBLISHERS

SAN DIEGO   NEW YORK   LONDON

ANNE LINDBERGH

ILLUSTRATIONS BY KINUKO CRAFT

▪ ▪ ▪

BAILEY'S WINDOW

Text copyright © 1984 by Anne S. Lindbergh

Illustrations copyright © 1984 by Kinuko Craft

All rights reserved. No part of this publication may be reproduced or transmitted in any form or by any means, electronic or mechanical, including photocopy, recording, or any information storage and retrieval system, without permission in writing from the publisher.

Requests for permission to make copies of any part of the work should be mailed to: Copyrights and Permissions Department, Harcourt Brace Jovanovich, Publishers, Orlando, Florida 32887.

Library of Congress Cataloging in Publication Data
Lindbergh, Anne.
  Bailey's window.
  Summary: When their grumpy cousin Bailey Bond accidentally creates a window to anywhere, Anna and Carl and their friend Ingrid are in for a magical summer of visiting faraway places.
  [1. Fantasy.   2. Cousins — Fiction]   I. Craft, Kinuko, ill. II. Title.
PZ7.L6572Bai   1984   [Fic]   83-18360
ISBN 0-15-205642-4

Designed by Dalia Hartman

Printed in the United States of America

C D E F G H

For Nathaniel Pendleton,
who already knows how to use his brains

"Do you want an adventure now, or would you like to have your tea first?"

—PETER PAN

. . .

BAILEY'S
WINDOW

Never had a car been packed so full. Not that you could really call it a car. It was a ramshackle delivery van with no backseats, and ordinarily there was plenty of room for three children and two dogs to roll around inside. Today there was hardly room to breathe. Cases and cartons, duffel bags, sleeping bags, tents, and tarpaulins had been wedged together like pieces of a puzzle, without an inch to spare.

They had been driving since breakfast, and everyone was tired. Mrs. Carlson was tired of handing out peanut butter and jelly sandwiches while she read the road map. Mr. Carlson was tired of kicking paper cups from under the pedals while he drove. The old van groaned as if it were tired of the road, and the children were even tired of quarreling.

"There's jam on the steering wheel!" Mr. Carlson complained. "Why do you kids need to be fed? These long trips would be so much easier if we could pack you up in trunks!"

Only two of the children and one of the dogs belonged to Mr. Carlson. Their names were Carl, Anna, and Leif the Lucky.

Leif was a golden retriever with a stub of a tail. He was old and fat and wore a tolerant grin from morning to night, sometimes even in his sleep.

Anna was ten years old. She had her father's Swedish flaxen hair, which she brushed back into a neat ponytail every morning before breakfast.

Carl was twelve and very serious. His thick, darkening blond hair tended to fall over his forehead when he thought about difficult problems, which was more often than his mother considered healthy.

The extra child was Ingrid Werbeski, Anna's friend. She was a few months older than Anna. Her dog was what friendly people called a mixture and everyone else called a mutt. "But at least she has a whole tail!" Ingrid would remind the Carlsons.

The van veered around a curve, sending both dogs into a yelping heap in a corner. Leif found an unfinished peanut butter and jelly sandwich and bit into it optimistically. Then he dropped it on Ingrid's lap.

"Yuck!" said Anna as she scooped up the remains with a napkin. "Everything is damp and smelly in here. Can't we stop for a while to get some fresh air?"

"We've stopped too much as it is," said Mr. Carlson. "Short of an emergency, next stop is home."

"Home" was in upper New York State for everyone but Ingrid. She lived in Chicago with her parents, but she had come to spend the summer with her grandmother, who lived a mile down the road from the Carlsons' house.

The Carlsons lived so far out in the country that most of their neighbors were beyond walking distance. Carl and Anna rarely saw other children, so they had learned to make do with each other. This year they had formed a club and called themselves the Vikings. But a club with only two members and a dog is hardly a club at all, so when they'd heard that old Mrs. Werbeski's granddaughter had come for the summer, Carl and Anna had been wild with excitement.

"How old is she?" Carl had asked. "If she's under seven she can't join. We draw the line at babies."

"I hope she's not a teenager,'" Anna had added. "Lipstick and boyfriends are definitely out!"

They had run down the road the morning after Ingrid's arrival and had been relieved to find someone their own age shelling peas on Mrs. Werbeski's kitchen steps.

"Are you Ingrid?" Carl had asked. "We're the Vikings, and this is Leif the Lucky."

Ingrid's grandmother had come out on the step to meet them. "I'm glad you warned me," she said. "Last time I saw that dog, his name was Sam. Why Vikings?"

"Our family is Swedish," Carl had explained proudly. "We all have Viking blood in us. Is Ingrid a Viking, too? It sounds like a Viking name."

Mrs. Werbeski had shaken her head. "Ingrid's family is Polish. She's no Viking. Her mother just named her after some movie star. Who wants a cookie?"

Mrs. Werbeski always kept an ample supply of cookies in her kitchen. She handed them out to the children whenever the slightest problem arose, a little the way their own mother handed out vitamins at the slightest sniffle. Carl and Anna always had room for a cookie, but Ingrid was not to be distracted.

"Sure, I'm a Viking!" she had announced. "And so is my dog."

Carl had looked doubtfully at Ingrid's dog. "What's his name?"

The dog's name was Squirrel, but "Squirrel" sounded even less Viking than "Sam." Ingrid had looked pleadingly at her grandmother and blushed before answering, "My dog's name is Eric the Red."

Mrs. Werbeski had kept a straight face as she dealt out

gingersnaps to three Vikings. She never again referred to Ingrid's dog as "Squirrel."

Squirrel didn't seem to mind being called Eric the Red, even though she was a female dog. She became fast friends with Leif the Lucky, and later that summer, when the Carlsons invited Ingrid on a camping trip, it was taken for granted that Eric would go, too.

Ingrid sighed happily as she thought back over the days she had just spent hiking, cooking over a campfire, and swimming in a mountain lake.

"I never had such fun in all my life!" she told the others. "And just think—there's still the whole month of August before I have to go back to Chicago. Isn't it wonderful the way summer vacation goes on forever?"

Anna was feeling carsick, which made her cross. "In exactly one month you start fifth grade," she reminded Ingrid. "A month isn't forever. The only thing that's forever is this car trip, and I warn you, if something isn't done about the smell in here, I'm going to throw up. It's hard to believe that this morning all you could smell was pine trees and wild flowers."

"And coffee and bacon and our campfire," Ingrid added.

"And wet sleeping bags and smoke and calamine lotion and mosquitoes!" Mrs. Carlson continued wryly. "I'll be glad to get home to a hot bath and an electric stove."

Carl stared at his mother as if she had just revealed a secret talent. "Can you really smell mosquitoes?" he asked. "What do they smell like?"

"She means mosquito *lotion*, silly," said his sister. "I don't care. There could be ten times more rain and mosquitoes. I still wish we'd stayed. Now it seems as if we'll never have fun again."

Mrs. Carlson laughed. "I thought Vikings were never at a loss for an adventure. But as a matter of fact, I have a surprise for you. Guess who is coming day after tomorrow to spend the rest of the summer with us."

For some reason, Anna was suspicious. "Nobody, I hope."

"It's your cousin Bailey Bond," her mother said, ignoring

her. "Your Aunt Frannie and Uncle Jed have asked us to take him while they go out to California."

"What is this?" Anna asked rudely. "Some kind of punishment?"

Mrs. Carlson sighed. "I know Bailey was a little difficult the last time you were together, but he's older now. I bet this summer you're all going to be good friends."

Anna looked so glum that Ingrid began to worry. "What's the matter with him? What's he like?"

"He's a pain in the neck," Anna grumbled. "He follows us around all the time, but he never likes any of the things we do. He's a brat, that's all."

Her father overheard. "That's not really fair, Anna. Bailey is a New York City kid, remember? He's not used to the crazy life you three live, running around wild in the country. I hope you'll try to make him feel at home."

"Chicago isn't country," Anna argued, "and Ingrid is just like us."

"But what's *he* like?" Ingrid repeated.

"He's Carl's age," said Mrs. Carlson. "Maybe a little younger. He and Carl will be sharing the attic room."

"Poor Carl!" said Anna. "I'm glad I'm not a boy."

Mr. Carlson was exasperated. "There has been enough discussion," he told Anna sharply. "Did you ever hear of giving someone the benefit of the doubt? You're a year older, remember, and Bailey is, too. It's going to work out fine, believe me."

Mrs. Carlson winked at Ingrid over her shoulder. "Don't you worry, honey. Anna is making a fuss over nothing. It will be fun for you to have another Viking in your club!"

Ingrid wasn't sure what to believe. "Why couldn't he go to California with your aunt and uncle?" she whispered. "I think people who dump their kids on relatives are cruel!"

It would never occur to her to compare Bailey's situation with her own. If anyone had accused her parents of dumping her on relatives, she would have been indignant. Ingrid loved every minute she spent with her grandmother, and it was a comfort to know that she would be waiting for her back at the farm with an open cookie jar and a hug that smelled of cinnamon and freshly ironed clothes.

"How soon until we're home?" she asked Mr. Carlson.

If the question had been asked once, it had been asked two dozen times since morning, but Mr. Carlson answered as patiently as he could. "Not much over an hour now, unless we run into some traffic."

There was no traffic. Exactly an hour later, the Carlsons pulled up their driveway and tumbled out of the car, hot, sticky, and exhausted, only to hear the telephone ringing shrilly in the house.

Mrs. Carlson fumbled in her purse for the keys and rushed inside, followed by Carl and Anna.

"It's your Aunt Frannie," she whispered to the children when she had answered the phone. "It's about Bailey—"

Anna didn't wait for her to finish. "Hurray!" she shouted. "Hurray! She's calling to say he can't come after all!"

Mrs. Carlson frowned and motioned for her to be quiet. She spoke for a minute or so and then hung up the receiver.

"When will you kids learn to keep your voices down while I'm on the phone?" she scolded. "What if Aunt Frannie heard you, or even Bailey himself?"

"Sorry," said Anna, "but what's the story? Is he coming or not?"

"Of course he's coming!" said her mother. "He's arriving a day early, is all. Bailey will be here by this time tomorrow. Carl, you'd better get busy and clear some of the clutter out of your room."

It was cool and quiet, with an August breeze stirring the dark leaves, but Ingrid didn't sleep well that night. She tossed around uneasily, listening as the clock in the downstairs hallway struck hour after hour. At last, toward dawn, she dozed off, wrapped in a cocoon of sheets.

She had gone to bed convinced that the next day would be horrible, so she felt insulted when she woke up to an ordinary summer morning.

"Weather is the rudest person I know!" she said at breakfast. "It never thinks about your feelings."

Her grandmother looked startled. "What on earth are you talking about?"

Ingrid took a large bite of homemade bread and chewed. "Today ought to be dark and stormy because I feel so awful. But instead, just look at it!"

The kitchen window was wide open. A warm smell of hay

mingled with the smell of breakfast, and the room was full of sunlight.

"Why are you feeling awful?" Mrs. Werbeski asked.

"It's that Bailey Bond," Ingrid explained. "Carl and Anna's cousin. He's coming today for the rest of the summer, and Anna says he's a brat."

Mrs. Werbeski laughed. "I remember Bailey," she said. "He was here last Thanksgiving, making a proper nuisance of himself. But cheer up! It's an ill wind that blows no good."

Ingrid loved the way her grandmother had a wise saying for every occasion, but she didn't think this one very encouraging.

"No wind at all is better than an ill wind," she argued. "I wish Bailey would stay home."

"Wait and see," Mrs. Werbeski advised her. "Maybe you'll change your mind. Meanwhile, don't get mixed up with Carl and Anna's problems. I always say, 'Don't trouble trouble and trouble won't trouble you.' "

The words had a soothing sound. Ingrid repeated them to herself as she tramped up the hill to the Carlsons' house that morning. Ten minutes later, she burst through their kitchen door chanting, "Don't trouble trouble and trouble won't trouble you!"

Carl and Anna didn't have to ask what she meant. " 'Trouble' should be his middle name," growled Carl, who was finishing his breakfast. "It suits him a lot better than 'Bailey.' "

Mr. Carlson was reading the news. There had been no papers on their camping trip. This morning he had a whole stack at his elbow and was shuffling through them noisily, with a look of pleasure on his face. When he heard Carl mention Bailey, he sighed and glanced up.

"Who is coming with me to meet the plane?" he asked.

The children groaned. It was a three-hour trip to the airport and back, and they were planning a meeting of the Vikings.

"It's much too nice a day to waste it in a car," said Carl. "We were driving all day yesterday."

"It's a glorious day!" Ingrid agreed. "I was just telling my granny that the weather is wrong for the occasion."

Anna giggled and Ingrid, noticing the startled look on Mrs. Carlson's face, became so embarrassed that she started backing toward the door.

"Seriously," said Mrs. Carlson, "I think it would be a nice gesture if you were there to welcome Bailey."

Anna squirmed. She was feeling a little ashamed of her rudeness about Bailey the day before. "I'll go," she offered reluctantly. "If no one else wants to, that is."

Carl brightened up, but his mother objected. "Why don't you both go? Then I won't have to bother fixing lunch."

"Oh, you don't have to worry about that, Mrs. Carlson," Ingrid interrupted. "My granny said I could bring Carl and Anna back for lunch. If Carl comes with me, he'll get fed, all right."

Anna's mouth dropped open. If she had known, she would never have offered to go to the airport, but now it was too late. Standing at the kitchen window, she watched Carl and Ingrid walking down the driveway, kicking up clouds of dust with their bare feet. She blinked her tears back so that her mother wouldn't know how much she minded.

"Your father won't be leaving for a while yet," said Mrs. Carlson. "Why don't you finish your sketch of the house while you're waiting? The cherry trees look so pretty in August!"

Ordinarily Anna never passed up a chance to use her paint box, but this morning she felt too glum. "I'm all out of green paint," she said sulkily.

"Then take a bucket and pick some cherries," said her mother. "We've left them so long they're almost gone by."

"All by myself?" Anna wailed. "It isn't fair!"

"It was horrid of Carl and Ingrid to go off alone like that," Mrs. Carlson sympathized. "Were they mad at you about something?"

"Mad?" said Anna indignantly. "They were grateful!"

Her mother looked at her sharply. "Grateful? What for?"

"For my being the one to sacrifice and go to the airport," Anna explained, a little smugly.

Mrs. Carlson sighed and sat down on the kitchen table. "Maybe I was wrong to say we'd take Bailey. He's been nothing but trouble for twenty-four hours, and he hasn't even set foot in the house yet! How about giving me a hand with these potatoes?"

Anna picked up a potato and started to peel it. "Is it too late to tell Aunt Frannie that you changed your mind?" she asked. "You could say we all came down with chicken pox."

Mrs. Carlson shook her head. "They're probably on their way to the airport already. Besides, I said we'd take Bailey, and I can't go back on my word. Is it really going to be so terrible for you? I know he can be a bit of a pest at times, but if you made a little effort, you might cure him of it this summer."

"How?" Anna asked.

"Oh, you know what I mean," said her mother. "When Bailey is being a pest, don't just run off with Carl and Ingrid. Take a few minutes to see if you can find out what's wrong. Put yourself in his place!"

Anna frowned and jabbed at the potato. "If you ask me, Bailey's place is with his parents."

"Maybe so," said her mother, "but there's not much we can do about it at this late hour. Promise you'll try, at least?"

Anna promised grudgingly.

"Good," said her mother. "Now, run upstairs and put on a dress. There's a seafood restaurant on the way to the airport and knowing your father, he won't be able to pass it by."

Anna hated dresses, but she loved seafood. For once she changed her clothes without complaining, and the food was worth it. Waiting in the airport for Bailey's plane that afternoon, she felt so deliciously full of hot buttered crab that for the moment Bailey no longer seemed a threat.

"There's nothing to be afraid of," she told herself as she felt with her tongue for the last shred of crab. "He's just a spoiled little boy."

It was a hot afternoon, and Anna was sleepy after her meal. She leaned against a window and gazed up at the sky. How could anything go wrong on such a beautiful day? Anna began to imagine the things the Vikings could do together if Bailey had changed for the better. She was in the middle of a happy daydream when someone dropped a suitcase on her toes.

"Ouch!" cried Anna.

Standing in front of her was a boy who, although he might be spoiled, was certainly not little. He was younger than Carl, but in less than a year he had grown to be at least two inches taller. His hair was the reddish color of polished wood, and he had bright blue eyes. He stared down at his cousin in a very superior way.

"Hi, there, kiddo!" said Bailey Bond.

Anna's toes ached so much that she couldn't talk. She was convinced that Bailey had dropped the suitcase on purpose.

"It's nice having you back again, Bailey!" said Mr. Carlson cheerfully. "Let's hurry home—it's hot as blazes in this airport. Anna, why don't you carry Bailey's raincoat? Bailey can take the small bag, and I'll take the two suitcases. Why so much luggage, Bailey? Planning to stay all year?"

"Not if you paid me a million bucks," Bailey muttered. He waited until his uncle was a few steps away. Then he winked slyly at Anna. "Hey, kiddo!" he said in a low voice. "Let's have that coat!"

"I don't mind carrying it," said Anna. "You have the bag."

"I'll carry the coat, too," said Bailey. "No trouble, kiddo."

Anna hated being called "kiddo," but she didn't want to mention it when Bailey was making an effort to be nice. She left the airport without noticing that Bailey had wrapped his raincoat into a tight wad and dropped it behind a bench. In fact, she didn't give the coat another thought until they were back home. Then she was reminded in the most unpleasant way.

"How's my favorite nephew?" Mrs. Carlson cried as she burst out the door and gave Bailey a hug. "You can go straight up to Carl's room and make yourself at home—or maybe you'd like some lemonade first. You must be thirsty after that hot drive."

"We're parched," her husband agreed as he pulled the luggage out of the car. "Don't go without taking something with you, Bailey. Here's your carry-on bag, and don't forget your raincoat."

He stopped short and looked around him. "Anna, what did you do with Bailey's coat?"

"Nothing," said Anna. "He took it back."

"Who, me?" asked Bailey innocently.

"You were in charge of the raincoat, Anna," her father reminded her. "Right, Bailey?"

"Right," said Bailey.

"But he took it back!" Anna repeated. "Remember, Bailey?"

Bailey shook his head. "Sorry, kiddo. You must have been dreaming. I had the bag, you had the coat."

Mr. Carlson looked reproachfully at Anna. "That was a little thoughtless. And you're the one who is usually so dependable!"

Anna glared at Bailey and ran to the house. When Carl came home at the end of the day, he found her in her room, tear-streaked and pale.

"What's going on in this place?" he asked. "You've been crying, Mom and Dad are all sour, and Bailey is going around snickering like an idiot. What's up?"

"Bailey's a rat, that's what's up," said Anna. "It's no fair! And no one believes me."

"Believes you about what?" Carl demanded.

"He took his raincoat back, he really did!" said Anna after she had explained. "He said it was no trouble."

Carl didn't think it likely that Bailey would be so thoughtful. "Maybe it just fell on the floor. It's awfully easy to lose things in an airport."

When she saw that not even Carl would believe her, Anna went to bed, although it was only seven o'clock in the evening.

Much later, when it was dark outside, she woke with a

feeling that something had changed. Then she heard thunder far away and saw a thin line of lightning in the sky. The maple leaves outside her open window had the heavy, damp smell that she had often noticed just before a storm.

Anna lay quietly and listened. Soon the rustling of leaves was answered by another rustling sound. The drops came down harder and faster until all she could hear was the comfortable pounding of rain on the roof.

As she was falling asleep again, Anna remembered what Ingrid had said that morning about the weather. She smiled to herself and whispered, "At last the weather is right for the occasion!"

Carl woke up feeling grouchy. He was all set to get up on the wrong side of bed except that, to make room for Bailey, his bed had been pushed under the window. Now there was only one side to get up on, right or wrong.

Carl didn't mind having his bed moved so much as seeing what had happened to his shelf. The shelf was, in Carl's opinion, the best feature of the attic room. It ran the entire length of the wall and, before today, had provided ample space for Carl's collections of bones, bottles, and unfinished chemical experiments. But the evening before, Mrs. Carlson had put a piece of red sticking tape across the middle of the shelf. She had made Carl move his collections over to one side. To the left of the red line was a crowded mess. To the right was nothing at all.

After unpacking the night before, Bailey had stashed everything away in the closet and his bureau drawers.

"If you're not using that shelf, can I have it back again?" Carl had asked.

"Sorry," Bailey had answered. "My friend Fox is mailing me his chemistry set, and I'll need plenty of room for it."

"Your friend *who*?" Carl had asked.

"My friend Fox. He's older than you, and a lot smarter. I was supposed to spend the summer with him, as a matter of fact. He was dying to have me. But it didn't work out, so I had to come here. His set has real test tubes. Not just a lot of old junk like you have."

Bailey was fast asleep now in the other bed. He had pulled the sheets around his ears until all that showed was a tuft of rusty hair. Nice hair, Carl thought in spite of himself. Almost the same color as Eric the Red's, come to think of it. It was a pity Bailey wasn't nice, too. Then he would share the chemistry set.

Carl dressed stealthily and crept downstairs. The more of the day he spent alone, the better.

Mrs. Carlson smiled as he came into the kitchen. "Good morning, Carl! How did you sleep? I'm afraid it's a bit of a squeeze up there in the attic."

"I was thinking of moving into the cellar," said Carl. "All I'd need is a sleeping bag."

His mother laughed. "Down with the spiders? There's no window there. It wouldn't be healthy."

"How about outside in a tent?" Carl asked. "That's healthy!"

Mrs. Carlson set a pitcher of maple syrup on the table. "How about giving Bailey a few days to settle in? You may find you enjoy his company."

"If I'm still alive," said Carl. "Are there any pancakes to go with this syrup?"

"They're on the hot plate," said his mother. "Leave half of them for Bailey, okay? He's a late sleeper, as I remember. And when you're through, come outside and give me a hand. I want to get the last of the cherries off those trees today."

When Ingrid turned up at ten o'clock that morning, she found the kitchen empty except for what she considered a very nice-looking boy stuffing pancakes into his mouth.

"If Carl and Anna hadn't warned me, that would be someone I'd really like to get to know!" she thought.

She was too shy to go in and introduce herself, however. Instead, she hurried around to the back of the house where she found the Carlson family picking cherries. She climbed up to the top branches to join Carl and Anna and was already hard at work by the time Bailey came outside.

" 'Morning, folks!" said Bailey. "Is it too late for breakfast?"

"You'll find some pancakes on the hot plate," said his aunt.

Bailey raised his eyebrows innocently. "Are you sure, Aunt Ellen? I looked, but the dish was empty."

"You must have looked in the wrong dish. Come on, I'll show you." Mrs. Carlson led the way into the house. A moment later she was out again, peering angrily through the branches.

"What do you mean by eating Bailey's pancakes, Carl? I've got enough to do this morning without mixing up another batch!"

Suddenly Ingrid remembered what she had seen earlier. "Carl didn't take them," she called down from her perch at the top of the tree. "Bailey ate them himself!"

"But he just woke up!" said Mrs. Carlson. "He hasn't had any breakfast yet."

Ingrid giggled. "Then he has a twin brother, and I saw his twin brother eating pancakes in the kitchen."

Mrs. Carlson didn't laugh. "Shame on you, Ingrid! You're the last person I expected to hear teasing Bailey."

Bailey intervened in a soft, pleasant voice. "Please don't get mad at her, Aunt Ellen. It doesn't matter. I can eat cold cereal."

He stared thoughtfully at Leif the Lucky, who was snapping up sour cherries and spitting them out again with a reproachful look on his face. "Maybe it wasn't Carl who ate the pancakes. Maybe it was that mutt. He looks kind of undisciplined to me."

Carl yelped and would have jumped out of the tree if Anna hadn't held him back.

It was all Anna could do to remember her promise to her mother. Secretly she would have been delighted if Carl had started a fight, but she forced herself to be friendly with Bailey.

"Come on!" she said. "I'll make you some more pancakes. I learned how to cook when we were camping."

"Anybody can cook," said Bailey scornfully as they went toward the kitchen. "My friend Fox can cook with his eyes shut! He can flip pancakes three yards in the air, and they never miss the pan. I bet you didn't learn to do *that* on your camping trip!"

Meanwhile, Carl and Ingrid were conferring in the cherry tree. They both thought that Anna was being much nicer to Bailey than he deserved.

"You know, I really did see him eating pancakes," said Ingrid. "He's just trying to get us into trouble."

"Like that dirty trick with Anna and his raincoat," Carl remembered. "And I was too dumb to believe her! I'm going to teach him a lesson."

"You can't," said Ingrid. "He's bigger than you are."

"Well, at least I'm going to stay clear of him from now on," said Carl. "What we need is a clubhouse or a tree house or something. And for Vikings only, if you get what I mean."

By the time Anna came back to help them pick, Carl and Ingrid had selected the perfect tree and designed a palace of a tree house in their minds, and by the time the last cherry was off the tree, Anna had imagined the perfect color scheme for rugs and curtains. They discussed their plan in low voices, because Bailey was picking halfheartedly in another tree.

"That oak tree is on your grandmother's property," Carl reminded Ingrid. "We'd better get her permission before we start building."

"Don't worry—she'll say yes," said Ingrid. "Come down and ask her after lunch."

Ingrid's grandmother had a real farm, not just a house with a vegetable garden and a few fields like Mr. Carlson had. There were a dozen milk cows, two workhorses, and a flock of sheep. There were also lots of chicken and geese, and no one, not even Mrs. Werbeski, knew how many cats lived in the barn, although Anna had counted seventeen the year before.

"Better go count those cats again," said Mrs. Werbeski when the children came to ask about the tree. "There have been a couple of new litters."

Anna dashed off to the barn, but Carl and Ingrid were not to be distracted from their plans.

"There's something important we wanted to ask you about," Carl began.

"Ask away," said Mrs. Werbeski. "How would you two feel about a brownie?"

"We'd feel good," said Carl, "but we really came to see about a tree."

Mrs. Werbeski set the jar down on the kitchen table. "Take some for Anna while you're at it," she said, "and where's that Bailey Bond?"

Carl's hand disappeared into the cookie jar. "We don't know and we don't care."

"We want to build a tree house so we can get away from him," said Ingrid.

"In that oak with the two low branches, next to the woods," Carl added. "Would you mind?"

Mrs. Werbeski looked at Carl in amazement. "Glory be!" she cried. "Isn't that just like children, to build a new tree house when there's a perfectly good one going begging!"

"Where?" Ingrid shouted.

Mrs. Werbeski laughed. "Didn't Dick and Ronald ever take you to their old hideaway?"

Dick and Ronald were the Werbeski children, only they had grown up so long ago that it was hard to think of them as children. Dick was Ingrid's father, and he lived in Chicago. Ronald had stayed to run the farm.

"Where's the tree house?" Ingrid repeated. "Show us!"

"It's away off across the fields," her grandmother told her. "Better wait until your uncle gets home. He'll know where that old rope ladder is, too. You'll be needing it. It's most likely out in the barn."

Carl and Ingrid hurried to the barn, where they found Anna sitting on a bale of hay with two kittens in her lap and three more playing around her feet.

Ingrid picked up a kitten and stroked it. "Guess what, Anna. My dad and my Uncle Ronald already built a tree house, and my granny says we can use it!"

"*Mmmm!*" Anna murmured with her nose buried in the kitten's gray fur. "I don't suppose she'd let me have it."

Ingrid stamped her foot with impatience. "Didn't you hear me? My granny says it's okay!"

Anna broke into a happy smile. "Really? Did she say which one?"

"What do you mean, which one? There's only one that I know of." Ingrid began to poke around the barn for the rope ladder.

"Only one!" cried Anna. "Why, there are seven in this litter and three darling half-grown ones that were born last spring!"

It was all Ingrid could do to keep from shaking Anna. "Glory be!" she shouted, because when her grandmother had said it, Ingrid had thought it sounded like a good thing to shout. "Glory be, Anna! Someone offers you a real, live tree house and all you can think about is cats! Come help us hunt for the rope ladder."

"Rope ladder?" Anna repeated. "There's one hanging up over your head."

When the Vikings went back to the farmhouse with the ladder, they found Mrs. Werbeski with her hair in pin curls and her arms full of wet laundry. She claimed to be too busy to give them directions to the tree house, but Ingrid wouldn't leave her alone until she changed her mind.

"You're a caution, Ingrid!" said Mrs. Werbeski. "You don't stop pestering folks until you get what you want out of them.

Don't you go breaking your necks, now. Maybe you'd better wait for Ronald."

"Don't worry," said Carl. "By the way, if you see Bailey, don't tell him where we are."

Mrs. Werbeski shooed the children out of her kitchen and pinned a stray curl back where it belonged. "You be nice to that boy and maybe he'll be nice to you!" she called after them.

"Glory be!" shouted Ingrid as they tramped across the fields. "The nicer we are, the more tricks he plays on us. I wish a tornado would pick that brat up and carry him to California."

The Vikings found the tree house at the edge of a field where Ronald Werbeski was growing corn that summer. It had a floor, three walls, and a roof, so they wouldn't have to do any building at all.

"It's perfect!" said Ingrid. "We can have picnics here. We can even pull up the rope ladder and sleep here!"

The three children climbed up and sat in a row, looking out over the fields. They could see all the way to the Werbeski farmhouse, half hidden behind the silo. They saw a speck moving a long way away, which Ingrid identified as her Uncle Ronald's tractor. They saw a truck go by, out on the main road.

"All the best things are happening to me this summer!" Ingrid exclaimed happily. "First I meet the Vikings, and then I get to go camping, and now we have our own tree house!"

"I wouldn't call Bailey a good thing," said Anna, "and he's going to go on happening until school starts."

When Carl and Anna returned home that evening, they found Bailey, his aunt, and his uncle sitting on the front steps.

Mrs. Carlson waved. "You two look cheerful. Where have you been?"

"I can tell you that," said Bailey. He spoke in a dull voice as if nothing could bore him more. "First they went down to the farm, and old lady Werbeski gave them some disgusting brownies. Then they went to this dumb tree house, and when they climbed up they couldn't think of anything to do there, so they climbed back down again. It's supposed to be a secret, by the way."

Carl turned bright red and clenched his fists. "Spy!" he shouted. "Rat! Only rats sneak around spying on other people. I hope you got close enough to hear some of the things we said about you. Serve you right if you did!"

His parents were bewildered. "Wasn't Bailey with you two? Why, we saw him follow you down the road, just after lunch."

"Who wants to follow them?" asked Bailey. "Can I help it if they happen to be where I go? What do I care about their dumb old tree house? I built a really good one back home with my friend Fox. It has running water and color TV."

"You see?" Anna exploded when Bailey had gone inside. "I know I promised to be nice to him, but how can you be nice to someone who spies on you and tells your secrets?"

Mrs. Carlson wrinkled up her forehead and asked, "Couldn't you have invited him to come along? If he really was 'spying,' as you put it, I think it shows he wanted to be included."

"Fat chance!" said Carl. "It's no use asking him to do anything. He just says he'd rather be doing whatever it is with his friend Fox. Am I ever tired of hearing about Fox! Everything we do, Fox can do better. But if Fox is so great, why does he like Bailey?"

"It's hard to imagine that boy having any friends," Mr. Carlson agreed.

"If he does, I suppose it's a pity he didn't stay with them," said Mrs. Carlson, "because he certainly isn't making new ones here."

The Vikings invited Bailey to the tree house the next day, but he refused to go.

"That chemistry set may be arriving," he reminded them. "Fox put it in the mail ages ago. I have some important experiments to do."

"That Fox!" Ingrid groaned as the Vikings walked down the driveway. "Why couldn't *his* parents have invited Bailey for the summer?"

But Carl looked a little wistful. "Fox can't be too bad if he's sending Bailey his chemistry set. I hope it's a good one. Not that it makes much difference. Bailey probably won't even let me look at it."

"Why is he sending it?" Ingrid wanted to know. "Why didn't Bailey just bring it with him?"

In any case, day after day went by with nothing more in the mail for Bailey than a postcard from his parents. Meanwhile, the Carlsons found Bailey harder and harder to live with.

Trouble seemed to crop up mysteriously wherever Bailey went, although it was rarely possible to prove that it was his fault.

Things finally came to a head on a Saturday. The trouble began before anyone was awake. Someone had left the refrigerator door open overnight. Curiously enough, the door to Anna's room, where Leif the Lucky slept, had been left open, too. Anna said she remembered closing it before she went to bed. But two pounds of cold roast beef had disappeared from the refrigerator shelf, and the dog was in disgrace.

Anna was furious. "You condemned him without a fair trial!" she cried. "You don't have a single bit of proof!"

"I'm sorry, darling," said her mother, "but I'm afraid there's no doubt it was the dog."

"He never did it before, did he?" Anna argued.

"Well, no one ever left the refrigerator door open before, either," said her mother. "The door to your room was open, too. It was pure carelessness."

Carl and Anna took some dog biscuits out to the garage to console Leif the Lucky, who certainly didn't show signs of a guilty conscience.

Seeing the dog gobble down the biscuits, Carl developed his own theory. "He wouldn't be hungry if he had just eaten two pounds of roast beef. You know what? I think he's being framed."

"What's that?" asked Anna.

"It's when someone arranges the facts so that people put the blame on someone else," Carl explained.

"Bailey!" Anna guessed immediately. "Do you think he ate all that meat himself, or did he just throw it out and leave the plate on the floor?"

"Plate?" Carl repeated. "I didn't know there was a plate on the floor. Was it broken?"

"Of course not!" said Anna. "If it had been, there *really* would have been trouble."

Carl jumped up and ran into the kitchen, where his parents were still eating breakfast.

"That roast beef was on the top shelf of the refrigerator!" he shouted breathlessly. "Leif couldn't possibly get it down without breaking the plate. So it wasn't his fault after all!"

Mr. Carlson looked thoughtful. "Carl has a point. Why didn't the plate break?"

"It *is* odd," said Mrs. Carlson, "but who could have done it except the dog?"

"Bailey!" said Carl fiercely. "He was trying to get us in trouble again. He opened Anna's door and the door to the refrigerator, and he probably ate all that meat himself."

"Nonsense!" said his mother. "Why would Bailey do a thing like that?"

There was no time to look any further into the mystery that morning because Anna had a dentist appointment and her mother insisted on her taking a bath, washing her hair, and putting on a dress.

"What on earth for?" Anna complained. "I went swimming yesterday. Besides, Dr. Irwin doesn't care if I wash my hair. He only cares if I brush my teeth."

"What's the use of putting on a clean dress if you don't take a bath first?" her mother asked.

"No use at all," said Anna, "so why can't I stay in my jeans?"

Anna was having lunch with her parents in town, but a picnic basket had been packed for Carl and Bailey. "Let's take it to the tree house," Carl suggested.

"No way!" said Bailey. "I'm waiting for the mail. By the way, I noticed your disgusting bottle collection is on my side of the shelf again. You'd better move it if you don't want me to throw it out."

"Those bottles aren't disgusting. They're antiques!" Carl protested. "People pay a lot of money for bottles like that."

"They don't look old to me. They just look dirty," said Bailey. "My friend Fox has some *really* old ones, back home. They're worth a hundred bucks apiece."

"Who cares?" asked Carl, not noticing Ingrid at the door.

"Fox cares," said Bailey. "I'm going to send him some more, too. I saw a whole bunch back in that old dump in the woods the other day, and they were twice as antique as yours. I'm sending them to Fox."

Carl jumped up. "Like heck you are!" he shouted. "Send our bottles to Fox? You just try!"

The old dump was a long way away, but Carl didn't care about that. Grabbing a sandwich from the picnic basket, he ran for the door. On his way out, he bumped into Ingrid.

"Hey, where are you going?" cried Ingrid. "Wait for me!"

Bailey watched Carl disappear into the woods. Then he smiled a secret little smile and turned to Ingrid. "I guess that leaves just you and me," he said. "Want to take what's left of the picnic to the tree house?"

"No, thanks," said Ingrid. "I just remembered my granny needs me back home."

"Aw, come on!" said Bailey. "I've never been up there, you know."

Ingrid was not impressed. "Why didn't you come when we asked you before?"

"Because those Carlson kids were so snotty about it," Bailey told her. "But you're different. Come on, kiddo! You can telephone your granny."

"Well, okay," said Ingrid. "But you'll have to hold the rope ladder. When it swings around, my stomach feels as if it belongs to someone else."

By the time Ingrid was safely in the tree house, she was changing her opinion of Bailey. He had been very understanding about the ladder. How nice if he had finally decided to be friendly with the Vikings!

"Aren't you coming up, Bailey?" she shouted. "It's nice and cool up here!"

The only answer was a dull thud on the ground below.

"Bailey!" she shouted. "What was that?"

"That was the rope ladder," said Bailey in a matter-of-fact voice. "I pulled it down."

Ingrid leaned over to see. The ladder was lying in a heap on the ground, and the ground looked a million miles away.

Suddenly Ingrid felt dizzy. "How are you going to get it back up again?" she asked anxiously.

"I'm not," said Bailey. "Tough luck, kiddo!"

Ingrid began to feel sick as well as dizzy. "Please, Bailey! I bet you could do it if you tried."

"Sure, I could," said Bailey, "but I'm not going to try. I'm going straight home to finish the book I'm reading. It ought to be a peaceful afternoon. You're stuck here, Anna is in town with my aunt and uncle, and Carl is hunting for invisible bottles in the woods."

"Invisible!" Ingrid wailed. "You mean you lied about those bottles?"

"It wasn't a lie," said Bailey, squinting up at her. "It was freedom of speech. This is a free country, kiddo."

"Not for people like you!" Ingrid yelled. "They put people like you in jail!"

"Who cares?" said Bailey. "I'd rather spend the summer in jail than with a bunch of stuck-up kids like you. You're always bragging about your dumb camping trips and your dumb Vikings and all the dumb things you do together. I wish I'd stayed home with my friend Fox!"

"I wish you had, too," said Ingrid, and she burst into tears.

Bailey never had a chance to finish his book because on his way up the driveway he met Carl, looking hot and angry.

"I hunted all over that old dump," Carl complained, "and all I found was a bunch of rusty cans. I cut my leg on one of them. I'll probably get lockjaw."

"That would be a pity, wouldn't it?" Bailey said sarcastically. "What were you looking for?"

"Those bottles you said you saw there," Carl reminded him.

Bailey raised his eyebrows. "Bottles? Are you crazy? I never said anything about bottles. You've got bottles on the brain!"

When Anna and her parents drove up a few minutes later,

Carl and Bailey were rolling in the driveway, hitting and kicking and pulling each other's hair. Ronald Werbeski had just arrived on the scene with Ingrid, who stood by with a dusty, tear-streaked face.

Mr. Carlson jumped out of the car and shouted, "Hey, what's going on here?"

He grabbed Carl by the seat of his jeans, and Ronald Werbeski grabbed Bailey by the collar. Together, they managed to pull the boys apart.

"Now," said Mr. Carlson, "what's this all about?"

Ronald Werbeski grinned and scratched his head. "Beats me! I found this little girl screaming her head off in our old tree house. I don't know how she got up there, but it sure took a lot of doing to get her down. She says that nephew of yours played some trick on her. I thought I'd come round and see what he had to say about it."

"I wasn't screaming," Ingrid protested. "I was just calling for help."

"How did you get up there in the first place?" Mrs. Carlson asked.

"Bailey helped me up the rope ladder, but then he pulled it down again and ran away!"

"Where was Carl all this time?" asked Mr. Carlson.

Carl's face was flushed and his nose was bleeding. There was one bad scrape on his right knee and another on his left elbow. He rubbed the elbow as he grumbled, "I was about three miles out in the woods. Bailey told me he saw some old bottles out there, but it was a lie."

Anna whistled. "Boy! I thought I was having trouble when Dr. Irwin drilled my tooth, but that's nothing to what went on here! I wonder what Bailey would have done to *me* if I'd stayed home."

"He seems to have done enough as it is," said Mr. Carlson. "Bailey, what have you got to say for yourself?"

But Bailey had disappeared.

5 Bailey knew that he was in for trouble, and he was almost glad. He had been expecting a showdown all week, but so far the Carlsons had disappointed him. The more he baited them, the more they left him alone. Even his aunt and uncle had grown distant and coldly polite. It all confirmed what he had discovered the day before leaving home: Everyone here hated him.

That last afternoon, while he was throwing odds and ends into his suitcase, he had heard his mother telephoning Aunt Ellen. "I want to discuss a few details about Bailey's visit," she had said.

Being curious about the details himself, Bailey had walked into the room just in time to hear Anna's voice quite clearly shouting over the phone, "Hurray—he can't come after all!"

He had pretended not to hear, of course. He had his pride. Besides, he had known there was no chance of changing his plans for the summer. But now Bailey was tired of pretending that he didn't care. He was also tired of inventing new ways to tease his cousins. He had a nagging feeling that it might have been more to his interest to have tried to win them over, but it was too late to start again. The best he could hope for was to be sent away.

"I hate this place!" Bailey muttered as he stamped upstairs to the attic room. "I hate this place and everyone in it!"

He flung himself on his bed and decided that he hated the Vikings more than anyone else in the world. What right did they have to feel so proud of their dumb club? It might not be so dumb if they let Bailey join, but they never gave him a chance.

"Nobody ever gives me a chance!" Bailey grumbled.

It was unfair. After all, he was a guest. People ought to be nice to him, but instead they shoved him around without even asking his opinion. Take the attic room, for instance. Why should Carl get to sleep next to the window while Bailey's bed was pushed against a wall?

The more Bailey thought about it, the more he put the blame on that window. It was mean of Aunt Ellen to let Carl have the window when Carl had so many things already. She'd be sorry when she came upstairs one morning and found Bailey suffocated from lack of air!

Bailey rolled over on his side and stared at the blank wall. He wished he could take a saw and cut a hole. The trouble was, there was more attic on the other side.

"Maybe I could *paint* a window!" Bailey thought. "It would be a lot better than Carl's window because Carl can't choose what he sees outside. I could paint the Pacific Ocean or the Grand Canyon or even skyscrapers if I felt like it. It could be a window to anywhere!"

Bailey jumped off his bed and ran down to Anna's room. He had done enough spying in the past week to know that Anna kept her paint box in the top bureau drawer. He could hardly wait to begin.

First he made an enormous frame, even bigger than the one over Carl's bed. Carl's window frame was green, but Bailey painted his black because Anna had run out of green paint. Then he painted curtains. Bailey thought they looked nice, and he stopped to admire them. There were no curtains on Carl's window.

But what should he choose for scenery? It was too hot for the Grand Canyon. He wanted something cool, like an iceberg with polar bears. Bailey started to sketch a polar bear and then changed his mind. There wasn't enough blue left for an ocean. There was still a lot of brown and white, though. Maybe he could paint a forest in the snow. Why, he could even put in some farmers getting syrup out of maple trees!

Most of the colors in Anna's paint box came in tablets, but the white came in a tube. Bailey squeezed a huge blob onto the brush. He used all the paint in the tube before he had enough snow. After that, he dipped his brush into the brown. With a dozen long streaks he painted a cluster of tree trunks. There was still some brown left, so Bailey drew a small log cabin with smoke coming out of the chimney. Then, to finish off the scene, he drew a man in a red and black checked lumber jacket, sawing wood.

Bailey sat down with his back to Carl's window and pretended that his own window was the real one. It wasn't a hard thing to pretend. The snow looked very cold. And when he sniffed, he really believed he could smell wood smoke. Bailey must be a better artist than he'd thought! But strangest of all, he could actually hear someone sawing logs. Back and forth, back and forth, until a hunk fell with a thud on the ground.

It was too real to be Bailey's imagination. Someone must be sawing wood outside. He ran to Carl's window and leaned out, but there was no one in sight. Then he stood close to his own window and stared. It was impossible, of course. He must be dreaming. But the man in the lumber jacket seemed to be moving. And that wasn't all. Smoke drifted slowly up into the sky. The snow looked so real that Bailey couldn't help touching it, and his finger came away wet. Not wet with paint—wet with snow!

Bailey didn't hesitate. He stood on his bed, threw a leg over the window frame, and jumped into the picture.

The first thing he noticed was the cold. He was standing in snow up to his knees, and all he had on his feet were sneakers. His arms felt cold, too, in his short-sleeved shirt, and a cold wind blew around his ears.

"Hey!" he complained. "I'm freezing!"

"Freezing?" repeated the man in the lumber jacket, who had stopped sawing to stare at Bailey. "You won't freeze on a warm day like today. Warm days and cold nights, that's what it takes for the sap to flow."

Bailey knew that the farmers tapped their trees in March, when the nights were still cold, although the days grew warmer. But Bailey had painted his window on the tenth of August!

"Is this March?" he asked the man in the lumber jacket.

The man had gone back to sawing wood and didn't hear.

"Hey, mister!" Bailey yelled. "Is this the month of March?"

The man took off his cap and scratched his head. "Um," he grunted.

Bailey hopped from one foot to the other, trying to keep warm. "If it's March," he asked, "do you mean next March or last March?"

The man didn't answer, and Bailey forgot his question because he noticed something that surprised him. There were buckets hanging on the trees, but he hadn't painted any buckets. He had drawn a dozen trees, and now there were more than he could count. And although Bailey had painted only one man in a lumber jacket, he could hear someone else moving around inside the cabin. He decided to go and look.

It was warmer in the cabin than it was outside. In fact, it was even warmer than Bailey's attic room on an August afternoon. The cabin was full of steam, and a dark liquid bubbled over the fire in a huge trough. A man was pouring maple sap from a big bucket into the trough and stirring it with a ladle. The smell was delicious.

"May I come in?" asked Bailey.

"Please do!" said the man. "I've been expecting you."

"Expecting me?" Bailey repeated in a dazed voice. "Hey, is this a dream?"

The man shrugged. "Does it make any difference, now that you're here?"

"The reason I'm asking," Bailey explained, "is that it's supposed to be August. You were probably wondering why I'm dressed in summer clothes."

The man looked up and peered at Bailey through the steam. For the first time, Bailey noticed that he had one blue eye and one brown. Bailey stared for a moment and then remembered that staring is rude.

"I don't think I'd feel the cold if I were dreaming," he continued quickly. "I wish someone would tell me if I am or not! If it's a dream, I can do whatever I want in it. But if it isn't, maybe I'd better be careful."

The man smiled in a way that made Bailey feel uncomfortable. "If you could do whatever you wanted, what would you do?" he asked.

All week long Bailey had been wanting to do the kind of thing you can't even do in dreams without turning them into nightmares. The tricks he had played on his cousins were nothing to the tricks he had planned in his head. But suddenly he was no longer in the mood for playing tricks.

"Could I taste some of that maple syrup?" he asked. "I'd like to find out if things have tastes in dreams."

The man scooped up a ladleful of hot syrup and walked outside. The winter wind felt even colder after the warm air of the sugar house. Bailey's teeth chattered so hard that he almost bit his tongue.

There was a loud sizzle when the man emptied the ladle over a clean patch of snow. Bailey tasted the maple-flavored snow with the tip of his forefinger. It tasted good. Good, but awfully cold.

"Do you know what?" he told the man. "I bet this would taste better on a hot day. I think I'll take it home."

He gathered the snow together so that it formed a bowl around the patch of syrup. Then a frightening thought came to him. It had been easy enough to get from August to March, but how would he get from March back to August?

"Hey, wait a minute!" he cried. "How am I supposed to get out?"

The man winked his blue eye in a teasing way, and then he winked his brown. "How did you get in?" he asked.

"Never mind how I got in. You wouldn't understand." Bailey squeezed his bare arms to his sides. The cold snow in his hands was becoming unbearable. "I want to go back!" he wailed. "How do I get home?"

The man laughed. Bailey could see the laugh coming out of his mouth in a frosty white cloud. It made him feel colder than ever.

"Why not follow your footprints?" asked the man.

Bailey knew that there were no footprints leading away from the sugar house through the snowy woods. At least, there weren't any his size. What's more, he suspected that the man knew it, too.

"Listen," said Bailey. "Do you know some kids that call themselves the Vikings?"

"Naturally," said the man. "I know everyone, and most of you better than you know yourselves."

Bailey was beginning to dislike the man, but he tried to be polite because he was desperate to get home. "Which way do they live?" he asked.

"Straight through those pine woods and down the meadow," said the man, pointing. "But I'm afraid you'll find that's not the way out."

Bailey had no idea what he meant, but he didn't care so long as he got home. Already, running made him feel warmer. He slowed down a little and jogged steadily until he came out of the trees and found himself on the crest of a small hill.

Down the hill to the right was the Werbeski farm. The Carlson house was a little farther up the road to the left. That is, there ought to have been a road between the farm and the house, but Bailey couldn't see it. No snowplow had been through recently, and there were no footprints in the snow. It was obvious that the Carlsons were away. What was he going to do now?

Bailey bit his lip to keep from crying. If only he had Anna's paint box and a place to paint, he could try painting a picture of the attic room. It might come to life, and then he could just jump back into August.

Absentmindedly, with the toe of his wet sneaker, Bailey sketched a rectangle around himself, the size a window might be if there were a window in the snow. Then he stamped his feet and shivered. It might be a warm day for March, but Bailey had never been so cold in his life.

Bailey closed his eyes to keep the tears from falling. To his surprise, it made him feel warmer. The icy wind stopped blowing and the snow seemed to melt away from around his legs. The air smelled of newly cut hay instead of wood smoke, and there was a stamping noise that sounded like feet climbing upstairs.

Bailey opened his eyes again and found himself standing on his bed in the attic room, holding a bundle of snow. Before he had time to put it down, Ingrid, Carl, and Anna burst through the door. They all wore angry expressions on their faces, but the anger turned to astonishment as they looked from Bailey to his window and back to Bailey again.

"Oh, glory, glory, glory be," breathed Ingrid. "It must be magic!"

After Bailey had disappeared into the
house, there had been a family discussion.
There was no getting around it—Bailey
had made life miserable for everyone since he had come.

"I've tried, though!" Anna had insisted. "Even though he's
called me 'kiddo' all week long."

"We've all tried," Mr. Carlson had said. "But it doesn't seem
to have had any effect. The point is, what are we going to do?"

"Kick him out!" Carl had advised without a moment's hesi-
tation.

"Couldn't he still go to California?" Ingrid had suggested.
"I bet he'd have a wonderful time out there."

"Personally, I can't stand him one minute longer," Carl had
said, "but if we're going to decide anything, I think he ought to
be here. Otherwise it isn't fair."

"Carl is right," Mrs. Carlson had agreed. "Bailey deserves a fair trial. Why don't you children go find him and bring him back to speak for himself?"

That is what they had intended to do as they stamped upstairs to the attic room, but they forgot all about it when they saw Bailey's window and the bundle of snow.

"Snow in August?" Ingrid said wonderingly. "It's got to be magic! And that painting looks alive!"

"How did you do it?" Carl asked.

Back in the sugar house, Bailey had felt warm and generous. He really had meant to take the maple-flavored snow home to share with the Vikings. He had even decided to apologize and make friends. But looking at their faces, he felt all the old feelings coming back again. They never shared anything with him, so why should he share his magic with them? He would never tell them how it happened, and it would serve them right.

Bailey threw the snow down on the floor. "Figure it out by yourselves, if you're all that smart!" he said, and he ran out of the room.

The Vikings sat on Bailey's bed and stared at the painting.

"That's Mr. Greenlaw's sugar house!" said Anna. "And that's Mr. Greenlaw's brother Ralph out in front, sawing wood."

"It looks like real snow!" said Carl and Ingrid together.

Anna touched the wall. "It isn't, though," she said. "It's only white paint. And I don't know why I said it was Ralph Greenlaw. It doesn't look like a man at all. Bailey isn't very good at drawing."

"That house doesn't look like Greenlaw's sugar house, either," Carl added. "Why, it's just a big blob of brown paint!"

It was true. When the children had come into the room, Bailey's window had still been alive. Now it had turned back into a painting, and not a very good painting at that. The only proof of magic was the snow on the floor, and it was melting fast.

Suddenly Anna saw something that she had overlooked at first. "Hey, that's my paint box!" she cried. "Bailey stole my paint box, and he used up all the white paint!"

"He used up all the green, too," said Ingrid.

"The green was already finished," Anna admitted. "But there's hardly any brown left, and he's gone and mixed the blue in with the yellow."

"That's how you make more green," Carl pointed out.

Bailey's aunt and uncle agreed that Anna's paint box was ruined. After they told him what they thought of his behavior, they made a list of jobs for him to do so that he could buy Anna a new paint box.

On Sunday Bailey cleaned up the attic room and washed his window off the wall. On Monday he sawed wood, on Tuesday he weeded his aunt's vegetable garden, and on Wednesday he washed his uncle's car.

Bailey worked without grumbling, and he played no more tricks on his cousins. He was too busy thinking about the magic window. The more he thought about it, the more he wanted to tell the Vikings about the magic, but they never mentioned it again. On Thursday he swallowed his pride and told them anyway.

It happened while he was mowing the lawn. Mowing the lawn hadn't sounded like a very hard job, but the Carlsons' lawn had a way of running off into the fields. It seemed to Bailey that the more he mowed, the more there was to mow.

While he pushed and pulled the heavy old machine, he could see the Vikings talking on the steps of the house. He wondered what they were saying. At last he aimed the mower toward the steps and stopped for a rest.

"Fox's father has a computerized lawn mower that runs by remote control," he told them. "All you have to do is turn the knobs on a little black box. Just like TV."

The Vikings looked at him suspiciously. Bailey never stopped boasting about his friend Fox, but if Fox was such a good friend, why didn't he write Bailey a letter? Even the chemistry set had not turned up in the mail.

"If you're sick of mowing, could I do it instead?" Carl asked. "I'm saving up for a ten-speed bike."

"Mother's birthday is tomorrow," Anna reminded him. "You said you'd help buy something for her."

Carl's mouth fell open. He had completely forgotten his mother's birthday. "It's too late!" he said. "Even if all three of us worked all day long, we wouldn't earn enough."

"How much have you saved up for your bike?" Anna asked. "We could pay you back."

"Nothing," said Carl. "I keep spending it."

"If your mother's birthday were in July, we could buy her some strawberries," said Ingrid. "They don't cost much."

"That's a big help!" said Carl sarcastically, "seeing as we don't have any money at all and this is August."

Bailey had been listening. Suddenly his face lit up with excitement. "I have some money!" he said. "And it ought to be easier to go back to July than all the way back to March."

The Vikings were astonished. Bailey had been gloomy and unsociable all week. Now he was grinning from ear to ear and offering to buy his aunt's birthday present.

"What do you mean, go back to July?" asked Carl suspiciously. "It's another trick."

"It's no trick," Bailey promised. "It's magic. I'll show you."

They left the mower on the lawn and stampeded upstairs to the attic. The dogs scampered after them, their paws slipping and scratching on the polished steps. When they were all gathered in the boys' room, however, Bailey's face fell.

"I can't do it without a paint box," he said.

Anna's smile turned into a scowl. "Nothing doing," she said. "Carl was right. It *was* a trick."

This time it was Carl who defended Bailey. He remembered the picture of Mr. Greenlaw's cabin when it had still been alive. "Come on, Anna!" he begged. "He can't make your paint box any worse than it is already!"

Ingrid agreed with Carl, which made two against one, so Anna went unwillingly to fetch the paint box.

"There's no more green and no more white," she grumbled,

"and there's hardly any more brown. I don't know what kind of picture he thinks he can make."

Bailey wrinkled his forehead and stared at the colors that were left. "What's the store like where you buy those strawberries?" he asked.

"It isn't a store," said Anna. "It's Mr. Kenner's farm, down the road. You pick the berries yourself and then Mr. Kenner weighs them and tells you how much you owe him. But they don't grow in August. All the Kenners have now is corn and cukes."

"Never mind that," said Bailey. "What's this Kenner guy like?"

"He's a grouch," said Ingrid. "He's tall and kind of skinny, and he wears a beat-up old hat."

Bailey drew a frame on the wall over his bed. He didn't bother to put in curtains this time. Who needs curtains on a magic window? In the bottom of the space he drew a tall, thin man with a large straw hat.

"Not like that, silly!" said Ingrid, who was looking over his shoulder. "It's not a straw hat. It's a gray felt one like Daddy wears to the city, only it's gone kind of droopy and it's not very clean."

"Stop breathing down my neck!" Bailey ordered her. He changed the hat.

"That's right!" said Anna. "Now make his mouth kind of sideways, as if he were chewing something that didn't taste too good."

Bailey painted a crooked red line. "What about his barn?"

"It's just like everyone else's," Anna told him. "You know, red with a silo. But his house is a funny color. Last year he painted it pink."

Bailey painted a big red barn with a silo. Next to it he began to sketch a house. "But I can't make it pink!" he said suddenly. "There isn't any white left to mix with the red."

"Whose fault is that?" asked Anna. "You're the one who used it up, not me."

"Just leave it out," said Carl. "Come on, hurry up and do the field."

Bailey smeared blue into the yellow to make green. Anna was horrified, but she didn't dare complain. "Put in some red dots for strawberries," she suggested.

Bailey put in some red dots and then drew a large sign saying STRAWBERRIES ON SALE—HALF PRICE.

Ingrid was shocked. "They're cheap already! My granny says you can't get them that cheap anywhere in town."

Bailey looked at her scornfully. "Who's paying for these strawberries?" he demanded. "You or me?"

"You are," Ingrid said humbly. "It's awfully nice of you, Bailey. It really is!"

Carl looked as if he were going to say something rude, but Ingrid jabbed him in the ribs with her elbow. She didn't want Bailey to change his mind.

Carl shrugged. "Okay, moneybags. Where's your magic?"

"What's your hurry?" asked Bailey. "If you don't like it my way, do it yourself!"

He was feeling a little less sure of himself. His new window looked like a very bad picture and nothing more. He began to wonder whether his adventure in the snow had been a dream after all.

Anna stared at her empty paint box and lost her temper. "I bet it was all a big lie about the magic!" she said. "You just wanted to use up the rest of my paints."

"Nobody cares about your paints," said Bailey. "Who do you think you are, Pablo Picasso?"

Anna jumped up and pounded him with her fists. "You're a monster!" she sobbed. "You're nothing but a great big bully, and you tell lies and you're mean!"

As Carl and Ingrid pulled Anna away from Bailey, the Viking dogs began to bark.

"Quiet!" Ingrid shouted. "Can't you see the fighting is all over?"

The dogs kept on barking. They glared at the painting on the wall and the fur bristled on their backs. Bailey's window had come alive.

The air in the attic seemed softer and a sweet, warm smell of wild flowers filled the room. The children could hear farm noises: cows mooing, chickens squawking, and the distant droning of a tractor at work.

"Shut up, Eric!" Ingrid scolded. "What's wrong, are you afraid of magic?"

Eric the Red stopped growling, shook herself, and bounded off the bed into the picture. It was strange to see her on the wall, a small ball of fur scampering toward the barn.

"Uh-oh!" said Ingrid. "We'd better go in and catch her. Mr. Kenner hates dogs."

Mr. Kenner was standing outside the barn, just where Bailey had painted him. He looked furious. "I *thought* I recognized that mutt of yours!" he snapped when Ingrid ran up. "Keep her away from my chickens or I'll shoot her one of these days."

Ingrid whistled for her dog and took a tight hold of her collar. "Eric doesn't chase chickens," she said.

Eric sat down panting, an innocent look in her eyes.

"What do you kids want?" Mr. Kenner demanded. "I thought the whole bunch of you were off on some camping trip."

Anna gasped. "He's right! We *were* camping last July!"

"Who's saying this is *last* July?" objected Bailey, who had been bothered by the same problem on his first adventure. "This might be *next* July!"

Mr. Kenner squinted at them suspiciously. He tilted his hat down over his eyes and folded his arms. "I don't know what tricks you're up to," he said, "but if you're not here to buy something, do me a favor and scram."

It was Bailey who answered. "We want seven dollars worth of strawberries, please. Ripe ones."

"Seven dollars!" cried Anna. "If you'd told us you had seven dollars, we could have bought something my mother really needed, like perfume or some jewelry!"

"You said she wanted strawberries," said Bailey. "Strawberries are what she's getting. I'm going to pick them all by myself, too. It's my present and I don't need any help."

Bailey could hardly believe his eyes when he saw Mr. Kenner's strawberry patch. To a city boy, it seemed to go on forever. Everywhere he looked there were luscious red berries peeping out from under the green leaves.

"Get moving," said Mr. Kenner. "I got chores to do." He plucked a long strand of grass and started chewing on it.

"Go right ahead!" said Bailey. "Just tell me where to find you when I'm through."

"Nothing doing," said the farmer. "I wouldn't want any of those berries to get into your mouth by mistake."

Bailey hadn't intended to eat while he picked, but when he saw that Mr. Kenner didn't trust him, he changed his mind. Keeping his back to the farmer, he popped one berry into his mouth for every three that went into the basket.

When you are trying to pick seven dollars worth of berries and eat one out of every four, you end up feeling fuller than your basket. By the time Bailey had picked five dollars worth of berries, he had ten dollars worth of stomachache. He decided to stop picking and go home.

Bailey expected to find the Vikings waiting by the barn, but there was no sign of the children and their dogs.

"If they wanted me to share the present with them, the least they could have done was wait," he thought angrily.

He didn't stop to think that the Vikings couldn't have gone home because they didn't know how to get there. Instead he traced a rectangle in the dirt road that went by Mr. Kenner's barn, stepped inside, and disappeared.

Ten minutes later, the Vikings came back to the barn. They were red-faced and breathless from running after Eric the Red, who had decided that it might be fun to chase a chicken after all. It had taken the Vikings half an hour to rescue the chicken and catch the dog. They expected to find Bailey with the strawberries, but he was nowhere to be seen.

"He didn't wait!" said Anna. "Now how do we get home?"

"Don't worry," said Carl. "I bet he's just inside, weighing his berries."

When they went into the barn they were met by Mrs. Kenner. "If you mean that kid who bought five dollars worth, he left a while back, and my husband's gone down to get the mail in the Plymouth."

This time it was Ingrid who was angry. "Only five dollars worth? I bet he went home to spend the other two dollars on candy."

"It was Bailey's money," Carl reminded her.

"Who cares about the money?" Anna wailed. "All I care about is how we get home!"

"What's the big problem?" Ingrid asked. "We're not lost. We can't be more than a couple of miles from my granny's house."

"Ingrid is right," said Anna. "We don't need Bailey's magic. Let's just walk home."

When the Viking dogs heard the word "home," they started trotting up the road. Luckily, Carl caught them before they had gone very far.

"You idiots!" he sputtered. "If we go home now, it will be last July!"

"Or next July," said Anna, remembering what Bailey had said.

"And if it's last July there won't be anyone there," Carl continued, "because we were camping."

"But if it's next July we *would* be there," said Ingrid. "What would your parents say, with three of us already there and three more coming in the door?"

"There would be four dogs!" said Carl. His face lit up with amusement at the idea. "I wonder if they would fight."

Ingrid took a firm hold of Eric the Red's collar. Whatever

happened, she did not want her dog to disappear into the future.

Meanwhile, Bailey stepped out of the picture into the attic room, hid the strawberries, and set off to look for his cousins.

"I've been looking for them, too," his aunt told him. "I can't find them or the dogs anywhere."

At last Bailey realized that they must have stayed in the window. He bounded upstairs and was about to step into July when he stopped a moment to think. He was the only person in the world who could bring the Vikings and their dogs back to the month of August, but they hadn't been very nice to him lately. What if he washed the picture off the wall? No one would ever know where they'd gone!

Then it occurred to Bailey that for the first time that summer, he had been close to enjoying himself. If he painted more magic windows, the Vikings might even let him join their club. He decided to bring them home after all, but to give them a good scare first. In the middle of Mr. Kenner's front lawn, he painted an enormous blue elephant.

It was a lucky thing that Bailey didn't paint his elephant on the spot where the Vikings and their dogs were sitting, because they would have been squashed. It was lucky, too, that the elephant was a friendly one, because rather than charge at the children he ambled off toward the strawberry patch.

Bailey was disappointed when he stepped into the picture. He had expected the Vikings to get on their knees and beg him to take them home. Instead they were laughing too hard to notice his return.

In a moment Bailey understood the joke. The blue elephant was pulling up strawberry plants and popping them into his mouth. He picked much faster than Bailey had, because he didn't bother to separate the berries from the leaves.

Mrs. Kenner was waving her apron at him. "Shoo!" she shouted hoarsely. "Git out! Shoo!"

Bailey would have laughed, too, if he hadn't seen Mr. Kenner's Plymouth coming up the dirt road in a cloud of dust.

"We'd better get out of here!" he warned the others. "Mr. Kenner might not think it's so funny."

When he saw the elephant in the strawberry patch, Mr. Kenner slammed on his brakes and jumped out of the car. After him came a man whom Ingrid and the Carlson children were sure they had never met before. If they had, they would have remembered, for he had one blue eye and one brown.

The stranger shook his head reprovingly at Bailey. "Blue elephants?" he said. "What next? Use your brains, boy. Use your brains!"

Bailey didn't stop to ask what he meant because Mr. Kenner was moving forward with a menacing look in his eye. Quickly Bailey pulled Anna into the rectangle on the road. Anna grabbed Ingrid, who was holding Eric's collar. Carl, with his arms around Leif the Lucky, jumped in last, just in time.

Mr. Kenner was surprised to see four children and two dogs disappear into thin air, but he didn't give it much thought. He had problems enough with a blue elephant in his strawberry patch.

 Mrs. Carlson was delighted with her birthday present. "Wherever did you find strawberries in August?" she asked as she poured cream on her second bowl of berries at breakfast the next morning. "I was in town yesterday, and I didn't see any in the shops."

Bailey winked at his cousins. "We didn't find them in August," he said mysteriously.

Carl kicked him under the table. He had a suspicion that the sooner you started hinting about magic to grownups, the sooner the magic stopped.

"Wherever you found them," said his mother, licking her lips, "they must have been very expensive."

That reminded Anna of something. "Why didn't you tell us you had money?" she asked Bailey. "You could have bought my paint box right away!"

"Nobody said I had to buy your dumb paint box with my

own money," said Bailey. "You just said I had to work for it."

His uncle frowned. "That's what I call splitting hairs. If you had enough money to buy Anna a new paint box, you should have bought it right then. It wasn't fair to make her wait."

Bailey thought how silly and unimportant Anna's sketches were, compared to his own magic windows that came to life. "How much have I earned so far?" he asked his uncle.

Mr. Carlson took a small black notebook out of his pocket and thumbed through the pages. "Four dollars and seventy-five cents."

Bailey looked surprised. "Why only four seventy-five? I make it five dollars!"

"I docked you twenty-five cents for not putting the mower away," said his uncle.

Bailey scowled at his cousins. Not that he really cared about twenty-five cents, but it was as much their fault as his own that he had forgotten to put away the mower when they rushed off to paint the window to July.

"Who cares?" said Bailey. "I'll buy Anna her silly paint box. But it won't be as good as Fox's paint box. Fox has one with gold and silver paint in tubes, and hot and cold running water for washing his brushes."

"If I hear one more word about Fox, I'm going to throw up!" said Anna. "I bet you made him up, anyway!"

The discussion turned into a quarrel, and before long Bailey and the Vikings were enemies again. That morning the Vikings went to the tree house and Bailey stayed home. The next day Bailey's uncle drove him to town to buy Anna's paint box, and the Vikings took a picnic to the lake. On the third day it rained. The Vikings packed another picnic and set off with the dogs to see if their tree house was waterproof. Again Bailey stayed home. He had bought a paint box for himself in town and could hardly wait to paint another window.

"Where should I go this time?" Bailey asked himself. "California? Or maybe to the moon?"

The moon sounded more exciting, and it would be easier to

draw. Bailey made a dark blue background and dotted it with yellow here and there for stars. He was just beginning to paint the moon when Carl burst into the room.

"Hey!" Carl yelled. "What do you think you're doing?"

Bailey scowled. "That's none of your business."

"It's my room!" said Carl.

"It's mine, too," said Bailey. "What are you doing here, anyway? I thought you were having a picnic in your dumb old tree house."

"It leaked," said Carl. "Where are you going this time? Can we come, too?"

"Thanks, but no thanks," said Bailey rudely.

"Magic is tricky," said Carl. "You'd better take us along so you don't get into trouble." He was surprised to see that this just made Bailey angrier.

"Trouble!" Bailey cried. "Who rescued you kids from Mr. Kenner and the blue elephant?"

Carl took a closer look at Bailey's new window. "What's that supposed to be, outer space?" he asked.

"I'm going to the moon," said Bailey. "Not that it's any of your business."

"What about your oxygen supply?" Carl asked. "There's no oxygen on the moon."

Bailey hesitated. The problem hadn't occurred to him.

"Listen, Bailey!" Carl said quickly. "It would be a lot more fun if we went someplace together. Not just me and you, I mean. The other Vikings, too."

"Fun for you, maybe," said Bailey. "Personally, I've had the Vikings up to my ears."

Carl sighed. "I'm sorry if we haven't seemed too friendly lately, but you've got to admit that you were just as bad. Let's forget it, okay?"

Bailey shrugged.

"Just think of all the places we could go," Carl pleaded. "Like how about if we took you to the forest where we camped? You'd love it there, believe me."

Bailey thought for a moment. He had to admit that life was more fun when he was friendly with the Vikings. "Well, okay," he said. "But I'll have to wash the moon off first."

Carl ran to find the girls while Bailey started washing outer space off his bedroom wall. When the Vikings came back with their dogs, Bailey had already painted a mountain lake and was working on the sky.

"I brought matches, just in case, and we still have our picnic basket," said Carl. "I borrowed the binoculars, too. I'll show you a couple of eagle nests, if you promise not to frighten the birds away."

"Too bad I didn't get Fox to lend me his binoculars," said Bailey. "They magnify seven hundred times, and they have three places to look through, instead of just two."

Carl was sure that Bailey was lying. "Then they'd be called trinoculars," he said. "What use would that be? Does Fox have three eyes?"

Bailey thought awhile before answering. "One of them works like a microscope. Sometimes Fox needs to look at things up close."

The girls exchanged meaningful looks. That boy Fox! They were beginning to hate him without ever having met him.

"Forget about Fox," said Anna. "Let's finish the window. You forgot the pile of rocks out in the water."

"How can I forget something I never knew about in the first place?" Bailey argued. "Do it yourself if you're so smart."

"Maybe I should," said Anna. "Just to make sure we end up at the right place."

Anna took Bailey's paint box and drew the pile of rocks. She painted some wild flowers, a cluster of pine trees, and finally, as a joke, some tiny mosquitoes in the sky.

"There!" she said smugly. "I guess that's about as close as anyone could get."

The children waited patiently for the window to come alive. After a few minutes a strange thing happened. First there was a woodsy smell. Then the lake water wrinkled into tiny blue waves that glistened in the sun, and small puffs of clouds drifted across the sky. But the wild flowers, the pine trees, and the rocks out in the water still looked painted, and the mosquitoes didn't move.

"That's funny!" said Carl. "The part Bailey did is alive, but the rest is still a painting."

Anna's face fell. Everyone had always said what a good artist she was. It seemed unfair that Bailey should be the one who could bring windows to life. But there was no arguing with magic.

"I guess you're right," she admitted. "Only Bailey can bring it alive. Unless someone else wants to try."

"No, thanks!" said Carl and Ingrid together. The only use for painting, in their opinion, was to make a change from harder subjects in school once a week.

Bailey felt swollen up with pride. He was master of the magic. Not the Vikings—only Bailey Bond!

Opening his paint box again, Bailey retraced Anna's rocks, her wild flowers, and her trees. Not being anxious to get bitten, he left the mosquitoes as they were. The picture didn't look quite as nice as before, but the rocks came alive with curves and shadows, and the trees began to sway.

"All ashore that's going ashore!" Bailey shouted, and he jumped through the frame.

There was an enormous splash and the next thing he knew, Bailey was up to his neck in icy water. Luckily he had fallen close to shore, because even if he had been a good swimmer, which he was not, the mountain water was too cold to stay in for very long. Bailey waded out shivering.

It didn't make things any better to find the Vikings on the shore, laughing their heads off. Even the two dogs seemed to grin.

"All ashore that's going ashore!" Carl echoed mockingly.

Bailey stripped off his T-shirt and wrung the water out. "That sure is funny, kiddo!" he muttered. "Next time I'll know better than to let you come along."

Ingrid grabbed his arm. "Oh, please don't be mad, Bailey! You'd laugh, too, if it happened to us, wouldn't you? And if you hadn't gone first we might have done the same thing. It's just that you made the lake awfully close to the frame, and then you jumped too far."

Bailey was too excited to be mad. "Let's explore!" he said. "Where do you get to if you follow that path into the woods?"

The others all had different ideas about what to do. Anna wanted to eat the picnic first, and Carl was anxious to look through the binoculars at the eagle nests.

"Oh, they won't go away!" said Ingrid. "I brought some marshmallows. Let's toast them over a campfire."

Bailey folded his arms and frowned. "Look here, you guys. It's my magic, so I think you ought to do what I want to do for a change."

The Vikings opened their mouths to object and then snapped them shut again. Bailey had a point.

"Okay," said Carl. "You're the boss. What do you want to do?"

Bailey looked around him. "All I want to do is explore a little," he said. "You've all been here before, so you can show me. Then we can have our picnic. All right?"

Anna was silent as she followed the others through the woods, and soon she started to lag behind.

"Keep moving!" said Bailey. "What's holding you up?"

"I'm hungry," said Anna. "I'm sorry, but I just can't go a step further if I don't eat something."

Without asking Bailey's permission, Carl and Ingrid sat down and opened the picnic basket. They gave Anna a peanut butter and jelly sandwich and took two for themselves. Then they remembered Bailey.

"Do you want some of my sandwich?" Ingrid offered. "There were only three, but we can split. Or you can have an apple. There are plenty of apples."

Bailey was hungry, but he was too proud to accept. "I thought you said I was the boss!" he pointed out. "I never said it was time to eat. Anyway, it's dumb to eat sandwiches when the woods are full of more exciting stuff."

Ingrid looked around her. "You mean nuts and berries? I don't see any."

Bailey shrugged impatiently. "Everybody knows about those. I mean things like chanterelles and shaggymanes."

Carl was impressed. "Do you know about stuff like that?"

"Sure I do," said Bailey. "Fox taught me."

The Vikings couldn't decide whether or not to believe Bailey. He might just be boasting, but he sounded very sure of himself.

"Which of those plants do you prefer, Bailey?" Carl asked cautiously. "The chanty ones or the shaggy ones?"

"They're mushrooms, not plants," Bailey informed him scornfully. "I happen to like boletus mushrooms, myself."

Bailey had never eaten a boletus mushroom in his life, nor either of the others he had mentioned. He just remembered reading about them in a book at school. He hoped that Carl would drop the subject, but he was out of luck.

"What are boletus mushrooms?" Carl asked. "Show me one."

Bailey looked desperately around him. "Oh, well, you know —they all look kind of alike. It takes an expert to tell the difference."

"Show me one," Carl repeated.

Some of the mushrooms growing in those woods were surely edible. The problem was, which ones? Bailey tried to guess which would taste less nasty than the others. The Vikings were looking at him suspiciously, and he knew he had better choose fast. He also knew that certain mushrooms were poisonous.

"That one!" Bailey said at last, pointing at the smallest mushroom he could see.

"Okay," said Carl. "Let's see you eat it."

The mushroom had no taste at all, but Bailey could hardly bring himself to swallow it. He remembered quite clearly that the book had said it was foolish to eat any wild mushroom unless you were absolutely sure what kind it was. He wished he hadn't boasted to the Vikings, but now it was too late. He wondered how long it took to die of mushroom poisoning. If he got sick out here in the woods, they might not find a doctor.

"That's it, kids," he said suddenly. "The fun's over. We're going home."

"Going home!" Ingrid wailed. "But we haven't made a campfire yet, and I wanted to bring some pine needles back to make a cushion!"

Bailey insisted. He warned the Vikings that once he went through the window, they might never get home.

"But why now?" Carl asked. "There are a million things to do here, and back home it's raining."

Bailey felt too worried to argue. "I'm expecting a long-distance phone call from Fox," he said. "Come on. It's now or never."

The Vikings were about to put up a fight when a park ranger came around a bend in the path. He stopped when he saw the children and stared at them with an amused expression on his face.

"Having fun, kiddies?" he asked. "Don't get lost! Don't start any fires! Don't eat any berries or mushrooms unless you're sure of what they are!"

Ingrid giggled and whispered to Anna, "Look at his eyes—they don't match!"

"That's weird!" Anna whispered back. "You know who else was like that? Mr. Kenner's friend—the man who was in the car with him that day we picked strawberries."

The ranger ignored the girls. "Wasting your time again?" he asked Bailey. "Use your brains, boy, before it's too late!"

"What did he mean?" asked Carl as the ranger continued down the path.

"Never mind," said Bailey. "I've had enough, and that's that."

Bailey sketched a rectangle on the forest floor and the Vikings had no choice but to step into it with him.

At the dinner table that night, Carl took a handful of mushrooms from his pocket and showed them to his parents. "Would you happen to have any idea what these are?" he asked with a meaningful glance at his sister.

Mrs. Carlson examined them closely. "Those are a type of russula mushroom. They're not poisonous, but some of them can make you very sick. You'd better throw them out. Where did you find them?"

Bailey turned beet red.

"In the woods," said Carl. "Are you sure they're not boletus?"

"Boletus?" said his mother. "Of course they're not boletus. Boletus mushrooms are spongy under the cap, and these have gills."

Bailey jumped up and ran out of the room. Mrs. Carlson thought he looked a little pale, and she was shocked when Anna winked at Carl and said, "I guess he won't die this time, but it would serve him right if he got sick."

There was a long-distance phone call that night, but instead of Fox, it was Bailey's mother, calling from Los Angeles. She spoke first to Bailey, who was still wondering whether he felt sick or not and hadn't much to say. Then she asked to speak to Anna.

"Me?" said Anna, running to the phone. "What on earth would she want to talk to me about?"

"Anna, darling!" said Aunt Frannie. "I know your parents would rather die than make a fuss, so I'm counting on you to tell me the truth. I have a feeling from Bailey's letters that things haven't been working out too well. Should I arrange for him to go somewhere else?"

For a moment Anna was tempted to say yes. Bailey's magic windows were a lot of fun, but Bailey himself was unpredictable. Just when you thought he had decided to be friends, he turned around and played a nasty trick. But suddenly Anna wondered what it would be like with Bailey gone. To her surprise, she realized that she would miss him.

"Don't worry," she told her aunt. "We're getting along okay now."

Aunt Frannie gave a sigh of relief. "You've taken a weight off my mind!" she said. "I know as well as the next person just how difficult Bailey can be."

"Oh, he's all right," said Anna. "But we're getting a little tired of hearing about Fox."

"Well, for heaven's sake!" cried Aunt Frannie. "Don't tell me Bailey is still fretting over that scruffy little dog!"

"Not a dog," Anna corrected her, "a boy. A boy named Fox."

Aunt Frannie laughed. "Bailey must have been pulling your leg, darling. Fox is a puppy that Bailey brought in off the street last spring. The poor little thing ran away a few weeks later. I offered to buy Bailey a new dog, but he wasn't interested."

Anna was too shocked to speak. She held the receiver away from her face and stared at it, paying no attention to the little voice that was squeaking through it all the way from California. Mrs. Carlson finally took it out of her hand and began talking herself.

When Anna turned around, Bailey was standing just behind her. His face was bright red, and he had tears in his eyes. "I don't care!" he blurted angrily. "You can think what you like and you can say what you like, but I just plain don't care, and anyway, it's none of your business!"

Anna walked away. She was still too shocked to want to argue with Bailey. Try as she might, she couldn't get used to the idea that Fox was a dog.

The next morning the Vikings held a meeting about Fox. At first Carl and Ingrid were angry. They said that jokes were one thing and lies another, and it would serve Bailey right if Anna had asked Aunt Frannie to come and take him away.

"But think how miserable Bailey must have felt," Anna said. "Just think how it would be if Leif or Eric got lost and people said we should just buy another dog."

"It would be awful," Ingrid agreed, "but I don't see what we can do about it."

"I suppose we could offer to find Fox," Carl suggested doubtfully.

Ingrid laughed. "Out here in the country? He got lost in the city."

"I know!" said Anna, and her face lit up. "We can use Bailey's magic!"

Bailey had avoided the other children all morning. When Anna went to find him, he ran up to the attic room and locked himself inside.

"Come out, Bailey!" Anna called, rattling the knob. "Please come out! We're not mad, I promise. We're going to help you find Fox!"

Bailey didn't answer.

"Listen, Bailey," said Anna. "You can't go back to New York City to look for him until September, right? But we could rescue him by magic right now, if you let us help you!"

The door opened. "Magic?" Bailey repeated. "How?"

"If you paint a window of where you think he is, we can go in and look for him," Anna explained.

Bailey stood back as the Vikings and their dogs filed into the attic room. He looked extremely embarrassed, and it didn't help when Carl winked and said, "I hear your dog has trinoculars and a chemistry set."

"Oh, shut up!" Bailey snapped.

"I'm sorry," said Carl. "Look, I think it's about time we made you a Viking. You've got the wrong kind of name, but I guess it doesn't matter. All that matters is finding Fox. Don't you agree?"

The Vikings voted unanimously to start out by hunting for Fox on the street where Bailey lived.

None of the other children had been to New York City, so they crowded eagerly around Bailey as he worked. By the time he had finished the new window, they were horrified.

After washing the mountain lake off the wall, Bailey had drawn a big, black frame. Inside there was no sky at all, just cars and sidewalks and apartment buildings. Everything looked dark and dirty, and there wasn't a tree in sight.

"Ugh!" said Anna. "Is that really where you live?"

"I don't mind living there," said Bailey. "It's fun. At least it was when I had Fox. There are lots of people around to talk to."

Anna peered closely at the window, which was beginning to come alive. "They don't look like very nice people," she observed.

"Some are nice and some aren't," Bailey explained. "You get so you can tell the difference."

The children had noticed that when one of Bailey's windows came alive, you could smell it first. Then you began to hear it, and at last you saw it move. The smells from the street where Bailey lived were so strong that Anna pinched her nose. There was a sour mixture of garbage and car exhaust, and soon they could hear cars honking and an endless rumbling of buses. There were voices shouting, footsteps running, and dogs barking far away. The children hoped that one of the dogs would be Fox.

"Come on!" said Bailey. "What are you waiting for? Let's go in."

The children slipped over the black frame onto the crowded sidewalk, followed by the Viking dogs, who immediately began to growl.

Ingrid decided that as far as cities went, she preferred Chicago. "Quiet, Eric!" she said. "Stop that noise and stay with me. If we stick together, we can't get lost."

They were well on their way to being lost already. The crowd had jostled and shoved them until Bailey, Anna, and Carl were almost out of sight.

Bailey grabbed Ingrid's arm just in time and pulled her into a quiet alley. "Do you think you could remember this place if we split up and met back here?" he asked.

Ingrid shook her head. "Can't I stay with you?"

"We'll find Fox faster if we go different ways," said Bailey. "Don't cross any streets and you won't get lost. Just walk around the block, and if you see a stray dog, bring him back here and wait for me."

"What kind of dog?" Ingrid asked.

Bailey hesitated; Fox was hard to describe. "Well, he's black-and-white," he said finally. "That's for sure. But it's hard to say if he's black on white or white on black. And he's on the little side of big, but he looks bigger than he is. He has perky ears, but when he's tired they flop over. And his nose starts out pointed, but it ends up flat."

Ingrid shut her eyes and tried to picture Fox. "Does he look like Eric the Red?" she asked.

"Not a bit," said Bailey. "He's just about as opposite as you can get."

With this in mind, the Vikings set off to hunt. Bailey crossed the street and disappeared up the next block. Ingrid, who was fairly used to city life, walked cautiously down the sidewalk in one direction, and the Carlson children moved very timidly in the other.

There were dogs everywhere, but all of them seemed to belong to somebody. Anna saw a Dalmatian who almost fitted Bailey's description, except that he was definitely black on white, and he was being walked by a lady who wore a hat with a veil. Carl saw a black-and-white spaniel with floppy ears that could have been Fox when his perky ears were tired, but he was on the small side of small and was tied up outside a barber shop.

As for Ingrid, she immediately saw a dog who looked like Eric the Red, and she was convinced it was Fox in disguise. Wouldn't a person capable of stealing a dog be capable of dying its fur? She was so sure she had found the right dog that she

unhooked its leash while its owner, a young man with a moustache, was buying a newspaper. Then she tore back to Bailey's
alley, arriving just as Carl and Anna ran in from the other direction, each with two dogs in tow.

From one minute to the next, Bailey's quiet alley turned
into a madhouse. The Viking dogs, who had not been happy
from the start, decided to voice their opinion. Their opinion of
five unknown dogs took a lot of barking.

Before the children could quiet down the dogs, the young
man with a moustache appeared, red-faced and panting, at the
entrance to the alley. He had brought a policeman.

"There she is, Officer!" he shouted, pointing at Ingrid. "She
just took my dog and ran. I couldn't believe my eyes—the nerve
of her!"

The policeman looked dubiously at the seven dogs and ad-
vanced with caution into the alley. "Hi, kids! What's the story?"
he asked.

Ingrid was too sure of herself to be intimidated. "We're
trying to find Fox," she explained. "Bailey's dog Fox."

"Which one of you is Bailey?" asked the policeman.

"None of us," said Carl. "He isn't here yet."

A crowd was beginning to collect at the entrance to the
alley. Some people were laughing and pointing at the dogs, and
others were just hanging around, hoping that something exciting would happen.

The policeman looked confused. Suddenly a small figure
elbowed through the crowd and shot into the alley. It was
Bailey.

"Hi, there, Sergeant Monti!" he called breathlessly. "How
are you doing?"

The policeman's eyes popped open. "Why, if it isn't
Bailey Bond!" he exclaimed. "I thought you folks were in
California!"

"Only my parents," said Bailey. "Not me."

"Are these kids friends of yours?" asked Sergeant Monti.
"What's the story with the dogs?"

"It's a mistake," said Bailey. "Remember that puppy I had last spring? He's lost, and we're trying to find him. But he isn't any of these."

Sergeant Monti scratched his head. "Sure, okay. The only problem is, how do we get them back to their owners?"

The young man with a moustache snatched up the dog that looked like Eric the Red. "This one is mine," he said. "And if you kids don't want trouble, you'd better lay off this dog-snatching business."

By now the entrance to Bailey's quiet alley was blocked, and it was all Sergeant Monti could do to keep the crowd away. It seemed to the Vikings that there were more angry dog owners than dogs, and they were right. When all the others had been claimed, there were several people left who claimed the Viking dogs.

"That red one over there belongs to me!" said a man in a pinstriped suit. "Hand him over!"

"It's a her, and she's my dog!" Ingrid shouted.

"Nonsense!" a woman snapped. "That dog is mine. I have her pedigree papers to prove it."

Eric the Red took one look at the woman and snarled.

Suddenly the others made room for a man in dark glasses. The man lowered his glasses to stare at the children, giving them ample time to notice that he had one blue eye and one brown. Then, replacing the glasses, he whistled. Leif the Lucky pricked up his ears and darted forward, wagging his tail. Bailey grabbed his collar just in time. He was very frightened.

"What are you doing here?" he asked. "Why are you following me around?"

The man in dark glasses backed off, smiling. "Use your brains, boy!" he said softly as he disappeared around the corner. "Use your brains!"

Anna couldn't take any more. She clenched her fists and burst into tears. "I want to go home!" she howled.

Bailey couldn't agree more. "Hold on," he told Anna. "We'll be home in two seconds flat."

Kneeling down, Bailey took a piece of chalk from his pocket and drew on the pavement.

"Hey, wait just a minute!" said the man in the pinstriped suit. "No one is going anywhere until you give back my dog!"

He reached out to grab Bailey by the collar only to find there was no more collar, no more Bailey, and no more dog. The Vikings were safely back in the attic room.

The more Anna thought about the street where Bailey lived, the less she liked it. In fact, she could not imagine how anybody would want to move there. It was crowded and noisy and dirty, and there were not nearly enough trees and animals to go around.

"What an awful place!" she told Bailey. "How come your parents go on living there?"

"It has educational advantages," Bailey said loftily.

Educational advantages rated very low in Anna's opinion. Bailey could get educated in the country just as well, couldn't he?

Secretly Bailey agreed, but he was too proud to admit how much he envied his cousins. "You don't know what you're missing!" he boasted. "There's all kinds of stuff you can do there that you can't do here. Like movies and museums, and every day I roller-skate about ninety miles an hour on the sidewalk with my friend Fox."

Anna's eyes popped open. "A dog on skates?"

Bailey remembered and blushed. "Sorry. I should have said that I went skating in the park a couple of times, and Fox came along."

"Well, we don't have anyplace to roller-skate, but in winter we ice-skate on the river," said Anna. "You can go for miles. And we go sledding. And Ronald Werbeski gets out his sleigh and hitches a horse up to it at Christmastime, and we go all over the roads, and I bet that's a million times more fun than your dumb old movies and museums!"

She glared at Bailey and Bailey glared back. Then they burst out laughing.

"Oh, well," said Anna. "You can have your city. If I were Fox, I'd run out to the country as fast as I could and look for the kind of place I liked best."

Anna's idea was welcome. Bailey couldn't bear the thought of Fox wandering around the city, starving to death. He tried to think what kind of place Fox would like best.

"Maybe a bone factory," he suggested.

"There is no such thing," said Carl. "If I were a dog, I'd head for a garbage heap."

Ingrid wrinkled her nose in disgust. "Why not a park? People are always leaving food in parks. I beg a dog could live forever on french fries."

"Maybe he went all the way to the ocean," said Anna. "That's where I'd go if I ran away."

"Fox has never seen the ocean," Bailey objected. "He probably wouldn't like it if he did."

"Well, what would he like?" Carl demanded.

"He and I are the same," said Bailey. "We like pretty much the same kind of thing." He stopped talking and began to dream of the kind of thing he liked himself.

It was Sunday, and the Vikings were walking to the church bazaar. The Carlson children loved bazaars. They gave you a chance to get rid of your own boring junk and then rummage through other people's junk where, with luck, you could find a treasure. Anna was carrying her old toy record player. Carl walked moodily beside her. He had tried to persuade Anna to let him turn the record player into a more useful kind of machine, but she had refused.

"Mrs. O'Conner promised she'd give me half of what it sold for," she said. "You're supposed to give things free, but she said she'd make an exception so I can buy something else with the money. Remember the clock I had that looked like a boat? I bought that last year for fifty cents."

Carl remembered. He had tinkered with it for days, but the clock wouldn't tell time and the boat wouldn't float. He considered it a complete waste of Anna's fifty cents.

The church was two miles down the road, in the village. There wasn't much to the village: a post office, one general store, a schoolhouse, the church, and a very small public library that catered mainly to what the farmers called "summer folk."

"Who reads around here?" Bailey had once asked rudely. "Horses?"

"Horses work," Anna had answered, trying her best to be even ruder. "*You* can go borrow a book if you like. It's not as if you were useful for anything else!"

Today, however, Bailey refrained from criticism. In fact, he was thinking how nice the village looked. Not only was there green grass instead of sidewalks, there wasn't even a real paved road. It was a nice, wide dirt road, and today it was lined with colorful stands.

Some of the stands sold food and others sold hand-knit scarves and sweaters. The best of the stands sold junk. Anna headed straight for a collection of objects that had only one thing in common: They all looked as if they had come from the very back of someone's closet.

Mrs. O'Conner was so pleased with the record player that she gave Anna two dollars. "Mind you, spend it here!" she called after her. "Profits are supposed to go for the new harmonium."

Bailey, Ingrid, and Carl stuck close to Anna because they

had no money of their own. Every time they saw something tempting, they would point out its value.

"You can buy eight books for two dollars!" Carl told his sister as they passed a stand where the librarian had set out a row of dog-eared books for a quarter apiece. "That makes two for each of us and we could trade, so it's more like buying thirty-two."

Anna didn't bother to question Carl's arithmetic. "No, thanks," she said.

Ingrid lingered at the kitchen stand. There were some nice teacups that would be even nicer if somebody washed them. "They would make a good present for my granny. I'd pay you back!" she promised.

Anna shook her head.

All four stopped at a food stand, but they finally decided against candied apples because it would leave them with only eighty cents.

"My granny knows how to make them," Ingrid consoled her friends. "Our apples are better, anyway. These are probably mealy."

They went on browsing. Carl wanted a steam engine, but it cost ten dollars. Anna nearly bought a knit coat for Leif the Lucky, but she remembered just in time that Leif hated wearing any coat but his own.

Then Bailey saw the picture. It was an old-fashioned engraving, in an old-fashioned frame, of a sad-eyed puppy staring at an empty bowl.

"Hey, look!" he said. "That's the spitting image of Fox!"

The Vikings examined it critically. "That's good art," said Carl after a while. "You see all those little lines? I bet that's hard to do."

Anna agreed. "I'll have this!" she told the woman who was running the stand. "If it's no more than two dollars, that is."

The woman liked Anna, but she didn't believe in lowering prices at a church bazaar. "I'm sorry, honey. It's three dollars and fifty cents."

Bailey stood up straight and looked her in the eye. "I'll mow your lawn or anything else you like if you lend us a dollar fifty," he offered. "I'll write you an IOU if you don't trust me."

Ingrid, Carl, and Anna were a little shocked, having been brought up to think that you shouldn't ask for money, but the woman laughed.

"It's a deal!" she said. "Here's your picture. I hope you enjoy it."

She put six quarters from her own purse into the cash box and wrote down her name and address so that Bailey would know whose lawn to mow.

There was what Anna called an upside-down argument about the picture. An upside-down argument is when you are so polite that you try to make someone else take what you really want for yourself. It's a little like grown-ups arguing about who should go first through a door, except that grown-ups don't really care about doors, and Bailey and Anna cared desperately about the picture.

"You take it," said Anna, pushing it away when Bailey offered it to her. "You're working for it."

"Only part of it," Bailey argued. "You paid for most of it."

"You saw it first," said Anna, "and it's your dog."

"Not really," Bailey said sadly. "It just looks like him."

Carl and Ingrid intervened. "Let's hang it on Bailey's wall, because that's where we go through the windows," Carl told Anna.

"After we find Fox the dog, Fox the picture can belong to you," Ingrid added.

Bailey's wall was looking very shabby. Four windows had been painted on and scrubbed off since he had moved into the attic room. Now the wall paint was beginning to flake away.

Carl hung the engraving in the very middle of the flaky patch. "This covers up the worst of it," he said. "With luck, my mother won't ask any questions."

The more Bailey looked at the dog in the engraving, the more he thought it looked like Fox. "You see the way his ears are beginning to flop over?" he asked the others. "That means he's feeling tired."

"Or maybe it's just that he hasn't had anything to eat," said Anna, looking at the empty bowl.

"I wonder why the jester doesn't feed him?" Ingrid asked.

"Jester? What jester?" asked the others.

"The jester at the back of the picture," said Ingrid.

The others looked closely, and for the first time they noticed a pale form standing behind the puppy. He was dressed in motley and a cap with bells, and he seemed to leer unpleasantly at the children no matter where they moved.

"That's funny!" said Anna. "I didn't notice him before. If I had, I don't think I would have bought the picture."

Bailey was quiet. He didn't want to frighten the others, but he was positive the jester hadn't been in the picture when Anna bought it at the bazaar. A shiver ran down his spine.

"I bet that jester *stole* Fox!" said Ingrid.

"Don't be silly!" said Carl. "It's just a picture. I bet it was made years before Fox was born. And who's saying someone stole Fox anyway? Maybe he just had an accident."

Bailey blinked to keep from crying. "It's no use thinking that," he said. "Let's just go on thinking Fox is in the most perfect place in the world."

"Where's that?" asked Anna, surprised.

"You said it yourself," Bailey reminded her. "You said a dog would go straight to the kind of place he liked best."

"Oh, sure," said Anna, "but I didn't say where it was."

"I didn't *ask* you where it was," Bailey grumbled. "You're the one who just asked *me*."

It was the sort of conversation that could have turned into an argument, but Bailey didn't feel like arguing. Instead, he picked up his paint box and started to paint. First he painted a bright red window frame, because red was a color that Fox had seemed to like. He painted a narrow strip of blue sky and a wide strip of green lawn. In the middle of the lawn he drew a large circle.

"What's that?" Ingrid asked.

"I know—it's a Ferris wheel," said Carl. "They have them at country fairs. Is it a country fair, Bailey?"

"Not exactly *country*," said Bailey. "It's in the suburbs. I don't think Fox could get all the way out to the country."

Anna looked worried. "It's no use taking us to a fair. We don't have any money, and we owe that lady a dollar fifty."

Bailey thought for a moment. Then he drew a large sign under the Ferris wheel. It said, FREE RIDES.

Ingrid jumped up and down with excitement. "What a terrific idea, Bailey! It's the terrificest idea you've had yet! Do you think they'll let the dogs ride, too?"

Bailey was feeling generous. In smaller letters at the bottom of the sign he added, FREE RIDES FOR DOGS, TOO.

There was still a patch of empty lawn. Having no use for empty lawn, Bailey put in five small booths with counters. On the first counter he painted candy apples, on the second a popcorn machine, on the third some cotton candy, and on the fourth a stack of ice-cream cones.

FREE CANDY APPLES! he wrote on the first booth. Then, going straight down the line, FREE POPCORN! FREE COTTON CANDY! FREE CONES!

Bailey frowned at the fifth booth and scratched his head. Finally he wrote in large letters, FREE PIZZA!

Anna didn't like pizza. "Could you put in some strawberry milkshakes?" she begged Bailey. "Then I won't starve."

Bailey couldn't believe there were people who didn't like pizza, but he added a sign that read, FREE STRAWBERRY MILKSHAKES! ALL YOU CAN DRINK FOR FREE! In tiny letters in the space left over he added, FREE BONES!

The first thing the Vikings noticed when they jumped into the suburban fair was the heat. There was no shade anywhere, and not a cloud in the sky. The children climbed into the Ferris wheel, hoping that going around like a fan would make them cooler. Anna and Ingrid sat with Eric the Red, and the boys sat with Leif the Lucky.

The wheel turned. It went around a dozen times before stopping, and when the children didn't get out, it turned again. All the other seats were empty, and there was no music. Ingrid thought a fair wasn't a fair without music. She began to sing and Eric the Red, who liked music, accompanied her with a howl.

From their seats at the other side of the wheel, the boys waved frantically. "Cut it out!" they shouted. "Stop that horrible racket!"

Anna was hardly more polite; she stuck her fingers in her ears. When the wheel stopped again, Ingrid and her dog got off. They wandered over to the booth that had free pizza and bones, and they were soon joined by the others, who were tired of turning around and around.

"It's a funny kind of fair!" Ingrid grumbled with her mouth full of pizza. "No music, no people, no nothing!"

"There's plenty of food," Bailey said. "What more can you want?" He felt insulted. After all, it had been his idea of the most perfect place in the world.

For the next hour, the Vikings did nothing but eat. First they had pizza and the dogs had bones. Then they ate two candy apples apiece and topped them off with cotton candy. When they reached the ice-cream stand, they were disappointed. There was no ice cream inside the cones.

"How dumb can you get!" Carl turned on Bailey.

"Me!" Bailey protested. "How could I tell there wouldn't be any ice cream?"

"You wrote 'Free Cones,' " said Carl, "so we got free cones. You should have written 'Free Ice Cream.' "

"Never mind," said Anna. "Ice cream would melt right away on a day like today."

The heat was growing worse and worse. No one felt like moving, except for the dogs, who were burying their bones. The pizza had been very salty, and what the Vikings wanted was a drink.

"It's lucky I made you put in milkshakes!" Anna told Bailey.

But the milkshakes were the thick kind that are easier to eat with a spoon than to drink with a straw. After the first mouthful, Anna made a face. "Yuck!" she said.

The others agreed. Even the dogs just sniffed at the milkshakes and panted reproachfully with their tongues hanging out of their mouths.

"What we need is some free water!" said Ingrid, laughing. "Maybe Eric the Red can find some. Water, Eric! Water!"

Eric understood. She sniffed around and suddenly bounded off behind the row of booths. The children dashed after her. To their astonishment they discovered a sixth booth, set by itself behind the others. An enormous water cooler stood on the counter. Behind the counter was a man reading a book.

"Excuse me, sir," said Carl politely. "Could we trouble you for a drink of water?"

The man turned a page.

"We're dying of thirst!" said Ingrid. "It's unusually hot for this time of year, isn't it?"

Bailey thought this was silly. "If it isn't hot in August, when is it supposed to be hot?" he demanded.

"Who says it's August?" asked Ingrid.

"Me," said Bailey. "I painted it August, so it's August."

"Oh, stop arguing!" Anna cried. "Look! Did you paint that, too?"

She pointed to a sign in big black letters. WATER: FIFTY CENTS A GLASS.

"Fifty cents!" Bailey exploded. "That's ridiculous! Water isn't supposed to cost anything!"

"I bet it's against the law," Carl agreed.

"It's unconstitutional!" said Ingrid, going one better.

They all glared at the man, but he didn't look up from his book.

"I never drew you in," Bailey told him. "You have no right to be here!"

The man turned another page.

"Oh, well," said Carl. "If you can't lick 'em, join 'em. Who has fifty cents?"

No one had a penny.

"Well, thanks anyway," Bailey said bitterly.

For the first time, the man looked up from his book. "My pleasure!" he said, and he gazed placidly at the children through one blue eye and one brown.

Anna gasped. "Him again!" she said, shuddering. "I don't like this place. Fox would have to be crazy to come here!"

Bailey himself suggested going home.

Mrs. Carlson couldn't imagine what was wrong with the children that evening. Not one of them would eat a single bite of supper. Instead they drank glass after glass of ice-cold water. And they looked so discouraged!

"Is anything the matter?" she asked anxiously. "What on earth have you been doing all afternoon?"

"We went to the most perfect place in the world," Anna told her gloomily.

"Yeah," said Bailey, "and the most perfect place in the world is for the birds."

"It was a dumb idea anyway," said Anna. "Even if it *had* been the most perfect place in the world, it wasn't exactly what you'd call a dog's paradise."

"Fox likes what I like," said Bailey stubbornly.

"Did you like the suburban fair?" asked Anna.

"It was nothing to rave about," Bailey admitted.

The Vikings had called an emergency meeting on Monday morning before breakfast. There was no real emergency, but Bailey, Carl, and Anna had all slept badly. They woke up long before the Carlson parents, and the meeting in the attic room was a good way of biding time until breakfast.

"Not that I could eat a bite of breakfast!" said Anna. "The trouble with free food is that it gives you free nightmares. I hope I never see another candy apple in my life!"

"It isn't really fair to have a meeting without Ingrid," Bailey objected. "Let's call up and tell her to come over."

"At six o'clock?" said Anna. "Mrs. Werbeski would have a fit!"

"Ingrid won't mind," said Carl. "She knows it's a race against time, to rescue Fox."

"If only dogs could talk, Leif the Lucky could tell us what kind of place *he* would run away to," said Bailey.

"Leif likes it fine right where he is!" said Anna indignantly.

"Fox liked it fine, too," said Bailey. "He didn't run away. He got lost, or maybe somebody stole him."

Early mornings can be chilly in upper New York State, even in the middle of August. Anna pulled Bailey's bedspread over her shoulders and tucked her bare feet underneath her.

"Maybe instead of running away he just ran *to* something he liked," she suggested. "What was Fox's favorite place in New York City?"

"That alley I took you to," said Bailey. "In the morning, when the garbage cans are out."

"Well, he wasn't there," Anna observed. "What was his next best place?"

"That's easy!" said Bailey. "Central Park."

"Then why don't we look for Fox in Central Park?"

"You think I haven't tried?" Bailey grumbled. But he stood up on his bed and started sketching on the wall.

Central Park, Anna admitted, did not look so very different from her own backyard, once you forgot that it was surrounded by skyscrapers. It was full of trees and flowers, and pigeons strutted in the grass. There were big children on bicycles and small children playing ball. On the whole, it seemed a fun place to go.

Carl, however, disapproved. "What's the use of going back where Bailey already looked?" he demanded. "If Fox went there, the dogcatchers would have gotten him weeks ago. Anyway, the leaves look kind of dirty and I can't stand pigeons."

"Pigeons are all I ever saw in Central Park, but I'll change them to something else if you like," Bailey offered generously.

Carl laughed. "You mean even penguins or ostriches?"

"Sure!" said Bailey. "You name it, I'll draw it."

"Okay," said Carl. "Make it a penguin."

Bailey painted a large black-and-white penguin under a tree in Central Park. Its flippers stuck out as if it were about to make a bow, and it had bright yellow feet that looked as if they belonged to a rooster, rather than a penguin.

Anna giggled. "He looks like a man in a tuxedo!"

"He is," said Bailey. "He's going to a ball."

He grabbed a pencil and drew a comic-strip balloon coming from the penguin's beak. It said, "May I have this dance?"

"You nut!" said Carl. "What it really needs is an iceberg. Penguins live in Antarctica."

"No ice or I'm not going," Anna told Bailey firmly. "It's too chilly for icebergs this morning."

It was much warmer in Central Park than in the attic room. Bailey had painted the sun fairly high in the sky, so if it was August, it must be close to noon, as Carl pointed out. In any case, it was too warm for the children to feel chilly in bare feet and pajamas. They felt just right.

"Let's split up and look for Fox," said Bailey. "We can meet back here."

"Nothing doing!" said Anna. "Remember what happened the last time? We'll stick together. And whatever we do, Leif stays with me."

She had tied the sash of Carl's bathrobe to Leif's collar so that no one would try to steal the dog.

Carl paid no attention to his sister. "Hey, look!" he shouted. "It's really there, and it's alive!"

Standing under a tree close by was a penguin that was taller than Carl—almost as tall as a grown man. The children stopped and stared.

As for the penguin, it stared back with a haughty expression on its face, opened its beak, and said, "May I have this dance?"

Leif the Lucky growled. This was the first penguin he had ever met, and he didn't like the looks of it. When he heard it talk, Leif decided the children were in mortal danger. He barked frantically, pulling at the bathrobe sash. Suddenly the sash came loose and Leif tumbled forward, landing in a furry heap at the penguin's feet.

Two things happened. Leif was so horrified to find himself at the feet of the strangest creature he had ever seen that he tucked his tail between his legs and fled. At the same time, the penguin gave a stifled croak, turned his back, and waddled away in the other direction.

Without stopping to think, Anna started chasing Leif. It was several minutes before she had caught up with him and retied the sash to his collar with a double knot. On her way back to the penguin's tree she noticed that she was attracting a lot of attention. Passersby were smiling at her. Many of them even laughed.

"What do they think is so funny?" Anna wondered. "I suppose they can tell I'm from the country."

She stopped to look down at her clothes and gasped. She was still in her pajamas! When she looked up again, she saw to her dismay that she had drawn a crowd. A dozen adults and twice as many children had gathered around her and the dog.

A young woman pushing a toddler in a stroller pressed forward eagerly. "What are you dressed up as?" she asked. "Are you one of those wandering minstrels? Can you sing us something?"

Anna giggled. "You wouldn't thank me if I did. I can't carry a tune, and anyway, all I know is 'Jingle Bells.'"

"Clown!" said the toddler in a decided voice.

"No, she isn't, silly," said another child. "Her nose isn't red enough."

The woman with the stroller looked more closely and frowned. "That's not a costume—it's pajamas!" she said. "Are you all alone? Do your parents know where you are?"

Anna tried to slip away, but the woman caught her sleeve. "Wait a minute!" she said. "Listen, I'm not trying to get you into trouble or anything, but are you sure you ought to be out here

by yourself without any clothes or shoes or anything? I mean, maybe it's none of my business, but Central Park isn't all that safe!"

"I'm all right, I promise," Anna told her. "My brother is just up the path and anyway, my dog wouldn't let anything happen to me."

The woman looked doubtful. "Well, okay," she said, "but maybe I'll just come along with you until you find your brother."

While Anna had been chasing Leif the Lucky, the penguin had drawn a considerable crowd of its own. Cyclists and joggers changed their course to follow it as it waddled purposefully across the grass.

"Where do you think he's going?" Carl asked, hurrying along behind.

"I don't know," panted Bailey, "but *he* sure seems to. You'd think he'd been here before!"

One of the joggers answered the question for him. "It must have escaped from the zoo!" he called to a friend.

"Oh, no!" said Bailey. "That's right, the zoo *is* in that direction. What do we do now?"

"What's wrong with the zoo?" asked Carl. "Maybe they have a pool for penguins. He sure needs it on a day like this."

True enough, the penguin headed straight for the Central Park Zoo, where it finally stopped near an ice-cream vendor, as if waiting to be told where he belonged. He caused such a commotion that two keepers came running, their mouths gaping with amazement.

"Hey, how did he get out?" asked one.

"He doesn't come from here," said the other. "We never had anything like that. Besides, look at the feet—there's something weird about those feet!"

"Well, we gotta do something pretty darn fast," said the first keeper, scratching his head.

"No, you don't!" said Bailey, stepping forward. "He's my penguin. I'll just take him home, thanks."

Carl tugged at Bailey's sleeve. "We can't do that, you nut!" he hissed. "Where would we keep him? He's better off here."

"I'm bringing him home," said Bailey stubbornly. "He can live at the lake."

The keepers stared at the two boys, taking in their bare feet and pajamas. "Hey, did you kids escape from some kind of circus act or something?" they asked. "What's the story with this bird?"

"He's mine," Bailey repeated firmly. "He's my pet. His name is—uh—Fox!"

Just then a third keeper came along the walk, pushing a wheelbarrow with two buckets full of fish. Ignoring the rest of the crowd, he grinned and winked twice at Bailey—first with his blue eye, then with his brown.

Bailey turned pale. "Don't say it!" he shouted. "Mind your own business! Use your own brains!"

The man winked again and said, "Your time is running out, boy. Your time is running out!"

Meanwhile Anna, followed by the woman with the stroller, had arrived at the penguin's tree only to find no penguin, no Bailey, and no Carl. She searched wildly around her, hoping to discover them behind a bush or a bench, but they were nowhere to be found. Then she looked back, saw the woman with the stroller waiting patiently on the path, and burst into tears.

"Oh, come on now!" called the woman as she hurried toward Anna. "It can't be all that bad! We'll find your brother for you, don't you worry."

Anna shook her head. "He's gone home," she sobbed. "Something must have happened and they both went home, and now I'll be stuck in this window forever!"

The woman raised her eyebrows but decided it was no time to ask what Anna meant. Instead she fumbled in her pocket for a tissue and wiped Anna's eyes.

"Listen, honey," she said. "Why don't you call home if that's where you think they went? Where do you live?"

Anna stopped crying and thought fast. If she let the woman

call her parents, it would cause a lot of trouble. Maybe it would be wiser to wait and see if the boys came back to rescue her.

"I'm staying with my cousin, Bailey Bond," she said.

Anna didn't know the number, but she gave the woman the address. No one would answer the phone, of course; Aunt Frannie and Uncle Jed were in California. But maybe while the woman was making the call, Anna could run away and hide.

"If that's where you're staying, we'll have you home again in no time," said the woman. "It's really close to here. Listen, there's a phone booth right up the path. You come with me and keep an eye on Jamie while I look up the number and call."

Anna stood by the stroller while the woman, inside the booth, thumbed through a telephone book. It would have been the perfect time to run, but Anna had promised to keep an eye on Jamie. Jamie was getting restless and was struggling to get out of the stroller. She was afraid he would tip it over and hurt himself.

"Hold still!" Anna advised him. "Your mom is coming right back."

Jamie scowled. "Zoo!" he shouted.

"Zoo who?" asked Anna.

The woman emerged from the booth shaking her head. "No answer!" she said. "Your brother probably hasn't had time to get home yet. Why don't you stick with me and Jamie for a while and we'll call again? I'm sure there's nothing to worry about."

Anna hesitated. Her parents had told her never to go off with a stranger. Besides, she didn't want to get too far away from the penguin's tree.

While she was making up her mind, Jamie began to squirm and cry in earnest. "Zoo!" he howled. "Zoo, zoo, zoo!"

"That's what he said while you were telephoning," said Anna. "What does he mean?"

The woman laughed. "He means 'zoo,' of course. I promised I'd take him to the zoo when we left home this morning. I guess he's getting a little impatient. Come on, let's go! We'll phone again in ten minutes."

Anna was unable to resist the temptation; she had never been to a zoo in her life. Feeling slightly more cheerful, she walked beside the stroller, answering the woman's questions as truthfully as she was able without mentioning the talking penguin or the magic window or the fact that less than an hour before she had been sitting on Bailey's bed in a farmhouse in upstate New York.

As soon as they reached the zoo, Jamie started up a new chant. "Ice cream! Ice cream! Ice cream!" he bellowed, pointing at the dripping cones some older children were eating.

"Not now, Jamie," said his mother firmly. "We have plenty of ice cream at home."

Again Jamie's voice rose to a howl. "Ice cream!"

His mother groaned and rolled her eyes at Anna. "You wouldn't believe what a mess he makes out of it," she said. "Let's find some animals to distract him. Look, what are all those people watching over there? Let's go see."

They arrived just as Bailey's penguin bowed stiffly to the crowd and croaked, "May I have this dance?"

The woman with the stroller gasped in astonishment, but Anna paid no attention. "That's Carl!" she cried. "There's my brother! Carl, where were you? Can we go home now?"

Carl was glad to see her, but he looked worried. "I'm all for it," he said. "I didn't want to come here in the first place, but Bailey won't go home without that penguin."

"Then let him bring the penguin!" said Anna. "Come on, let's go!"

"Wait a moment, sweetheart!" said one of the keepers. "I'm not sure he can do that."

"Of course he can!" said Anna impatiently. "He drew him, didn't he? He drew this place and all the people in it. He can do what he likes with the whole bunch of you—none of you are real anyway!"

There was a moment of silence. Slowly the crowd drew closer.

"Now you've done it!" said Bailey. As fast as possible, he

traced an invisible rectangle around himself, his cousins, and their dog. All four were back in the attic room before Bailey realized that he had forgotten to include the penguin.

"You brat!" Bailey shouted at Anna when he had caught his breath. "You numbskull! You ruined everything!"

"I'm sorry, Bailey," Anna said humbly. "I didn't think what I was saying. Can't we go back and rescue the penguin?"

"The picture is dying," said Bailey. "Look!"

As the children watched, the colors dulled, the smells vanished, and the people ceased to move. Only a faraway croaking lingered a moment in the attic room: "May I have this dance?"

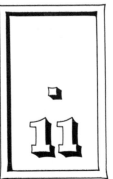

11 "What do you suppose would happen," Carl wondered, "if Bailey drew a window of our house last year, and we went through, and Bailey drew another window of our house the year before, and we went through again, and he drew another window of the year before that—"

"Nothing would happen," Bailey said flatly, "because I just wouldn't."

"But what would happen if you *did?*"

The Vikings were sprawled lazily on the tree-house floor, looking down at the field where Ronald Werbeski was riding on his tractor. It was a hot afternoon without a cloud in the sky. They were wearing their bathing suits under their clothes because they meant to go swimming, but it was a long, hot walk to the lake.

"It would be like mirrors," said Anna in answer to Carl's

question. "When there's one behind you and one in front of you, and you can see yourself forever in both directions."

"If you went back too far, we wouldn't be here," said Carl. "We didn't move in until I was four."

"Let's go back and see who lived here before!" Ingrid suggested excitedly.

"No, let's go forward," said Carl. "Let's draw a window of the house a hundred years from now and see what it's like."

"Let's not," said Anna. "Mother and Daddy would have white hair and beards and Leif the Lucky might be dead. Besides, if you don't know what it's like a hundred years from now, how can you draw it?"

"Fox wouldn't be there," said Bailey, "so it would be a waste of time."

It was much too hot to start an argument by reminding Bailey that in the week following their visit to Central Park he had painted three different windows, in none of which was there the slightest hope of finding Fox.

One stifling afternoon they had gone sledding in December. Bailey had painted Christmas Day, and when they came inside after sledding, they had found a Christmas tree with presents piled under it. The Vikings had felt as if they were trespassing and had decided not to open anything.

"Because if we took the things home," Anna had pointed out, "what would happen to the other me when I came down-stairs and the presents were gone?"

Another day the Vikings had decided to visit one another's schools. After painting yellow, red, and orange maple leaves to set the scene for autumn, Bailey had drawn the village school-house with a bushel basket of ripe apples outside the door.

The teacher had not been happy when four children eating apples had tramped into the middle of her history lesson. Carl and Anna, catching sight of another Carl and another Anna sitting at their desks, had felt too spooky to stay.

Afterward, Bailey had taken the Vikings and their dogs to

his own school in New York City. Although they had not expected to like it there, they had all had a good time and were disappointed when Bailey's teacher made them go away. The class was so big that she might not have noticed a few extra children, but no one could help but notice two dogs howling in the middle of a music lesson.

"We were crazy to waste a summer day going to school!" said Ingrid, remembering. "It's bad enough having to go all winter."

"At least that man with the funny eyes wasn't there," said Bailey. "I'm tired of being told to use my brains."

Suddenly he caught his breath. "The last time I saw him, he told me my time was running out. I wonder what he meant."

"He probably meant that if we didn't hurry, it would be too late to rescue Fox," said Carl gloomily. "But what can we do? It's like looking for a needle in a haystack!"

"Well, let's go for a swim before we go home for supper," said Anna. "It's already getting dark."

"Are you crazy?" said Carl. "It's only four o'clock. It can't be getting dark."

There was a loud shout from below. The Vikings leaned out and saw Ronald Werbeski peering up at them through the branches.

"You kids better get down from that tree before lightning hits it!" he shouted. "There's a storm coming, and it's going to be a gooder!"

The first heavy drops began to fall when they were halfway across the next field. There was a rumble of thunder, and a strong smell of dust rose from the ground. The rain felt good at first, but soon it grew colder and heavier. By the time the Vikings were racing up the driveway, the rain had turned to hail. Big, icy nuggets sent the dogs scuttling into the dark space under the front porch.

"Bad for the crops!" said Mrs. Carlson as she held open the door. "You'd better run upstairs and change."

Even with dry clothes, the children felt chilly. It was hard to believe that only half an hour before they had been too hot to walk to the lake.

"Where I'd like to be right now is Florida!" said Bailey, hugging his arms around his chest.

"Or the Sahara Desert!" said Carl.

"The dogs would hate the Sahara Desert," Anna objected. "There isn't any water, and the sand would burn their paws."

"How about a south sea island?" Ingrid suggested. "The ocean all around you, and a fresh spring running out of the jungle, and bananas and coconuts to eat."

"And snakes and tarantulas!" Anna added cynically. She was beginning to mistrust Bailey's windows.

"He wouldn't have to draw in any snakes or tarantulas," said Ingrid.

"I don't have to draw anything at all," said Bailey. Still, it was an attractive thought. He picked up his paint box and set to work.

Although he was not much of an artist, Bailey had always enjoyed drawing palm trees. He drew thick clusters of them all over the island, with bananas and coconuts among the leaves.

Ingrid giggled. "You've got bananas and coconuts growing on the same trees, silly!"

"That's right," said Bailey. "They're coconana trees." He drew a few bunches of bananas on the ground, in case the others were out of reach.

"Let's have some monkeys," Carl suggested. "Small ones that wouldn't bother strangers."

Bailey added seven monkeys and the head and neck of a giraffe looking over the leaves. Last of all, just for fun, he painted two mysterious eyes peering out of the shadows.

"What's that?" asked Anna.

"You name it!" said Bailey. "Come on, let's go!"

This time Bailey had drawn the beach right up to the window frame, so there was no danger of falling into the ocean by mistake. The Vikings jumped on the sand and breathed in large gulps of fragrant, tropical air.

"This is fabulous!" said Ingrid. "This is the best window you've ever made!"

The sun was hot, but there was a cool breeze blowing. The coconana palms swayed gently. Clear green waves lapped softly at the shore. A friendly chattering of birds and monkeys drifted down from the trees.

The Vikings ate bananas and found them much tastier than the ones their parents bought in stores. They cracked open a coconut and pried out the meat. They drank the fresh spring water that ran out from under the trees. They went swimming and met none of the dangers that the magic might have put in as a trick: no undertow, no sharks, no sharp coral to cut their feet.

"I have nothing against fairs," said Anna when they were drying off on the beach, "but in my opinion, *this* is the most perfect place in the world."

Bailey agreed. "Fox would like it, too," he said. "This is where he'd be if he knew how to get here."

"It's too bad we ever have to go home," said Carl.

"Let's not!" said Ingrid. "Let's spend the night here."

"I could spend my whole life here," said Anna, "just swimming and lying in the sun and eating bananas."

Bailey stood up. "I'm sick of bananas. Let's explore! Maybe we'll find a diamond mine or buried treasure. Who knows—we might even find Fox!"

Ingrid groaned and Anna grumbled. Even the dogs were too comfortable to move.

"Forget it!" said Bailey. "I'll go by myself."

Without waiting a moment longer, he marched off through the trees.

"We'd better go after him," Carl said sleepily. "When there's magic around, it's safer to stick together. After all, he's my cousin."

By the time they put on their socks and laced up their

sneakers, Bailey was out of sight. He had found a path leading through the coconana palms. Soon the trees thickened into a jungle and the path became narrower. There were so many vines and creepers growing overhead that the sun no longer filtered through the leaves, and it was almost as dark as night.

Bailey began to wish he had stayed with the others on the beach. Suddenly he turned a corner and gasped. Peering out of the shadows just ahead of him were the two mysterious eyes that he had painted as a joke on his bedroom wall.

Bailey stopped short, swung around, and ran as fast as he could in the opposite direction. He waited until he had turned another corner before dodging behind a tree. When he was sure that no one had seen him stop, he climbed the tree and held his breath.

Nothing happened. No one went by on the path, and for a moment the jungle was silent. Bailey wasn't sure whether the eyes had belonged to a man or to a wild beast until he heard a muffled beating of drums, not far away.

Cannibals! thought Bailey, and his blood ran cold.

Meanwhile it had not taken the other children long to discover which way Bailey had gone. Even if they had not found the path, the dogs were trotting along with their noses to the ground, showing them the way. As they went by his tree, Bailey tried to call out and warn them, but it was too late. They walked right into the trap.

Out of the shadows jumped a whole tribe of the strangest-looking people Bailey had ever seen in his life. Their skin was green, and they were naked except for necklaces of shells. Their hair was blue and tied on top of their heads in lumpy knots around large bones. Bailey suspected they were human bones.

When Anna saw the cannibals, she screamed. Carl grabbed her arm and held it tight. Ingrid caught Eric the Red by the collar, and both dogs growled.

"Don't panic!" Carl whispered in a shaky voice. "Don't let them think you're scared. Maybe they're friendly, who knows?"

The girls knew. They had never seen such unfriendly-looking people in their lives.

"The important thing is to communicate with them and show that we don't mean to do them any harm," Carl continued.

Ingrid couldn't imagine what harm the children could do even if they meant to, but she nodded bravely.

"That one must be the chief," said Carl, nodding at a cannibal who was standing in the foreground. "He's wearing more necklaces than the others."

He stepped forward and held out his right hand. "How do you do?" he said in a loud voice. "We are friends from across the sea."

"*Buroomba lumba boo!*" the cannibal chief replied rudely.

"He doesn't speak English," Carl told the girls. "Let's try French."

Anna knew only one thing to say in French: "*Bonjour, Madame!*"

"*Buroomba gurrawurrawurra*," snarled the cannibal chief.

"*Pan móvi po polsku?*" Ingrid piped up unexpectedly, and then she blushed.

"*Lumba!*" shouted the cannibal chief. "*Lumba hoooo!*"

He thumped the palm of his left hand three times with a bone. It was obviously an order to the tribe, because the Vikings found themselves surrounded. Before they knew it, they were all tied solidly to the trunk of a tree. It happened to be Bailey's tree.

Bailey slithered down until he came close enough to whisper and be heard. "Are you okay?" he asked.

Ingrid thought it was Carl whispering. "Of course I'm not okay, and neither are you!" she answered crossly.

"Shhh!" said Bailey. "It's me! I'm up here! But don't look or they'll find me too."

The children tried their hardest not to look. "Oh, Bailey!" said Anna. "Will they eat us? What are we going to do?"

"It doesn't look as if *you* can do much," Bailey whispered.

"I'll have to do something myself. I can't wait to get my hands on that chief. Did you notice his eyes? It's the same guy again. I'm going to shut him up forever, before he gets a chance to make another crack about my brains."

"I wouldn't try anything," said Carl. "He's much bigger than you are, and he has a whole tribe to protect him."

"If only we had something to bribe them with," said Ingrid. "You know: pretty beads or cigarette lighters."

"What good would that do?" asked Anna. "They'd just take the stuff and eat us anyway."

"How about threatening them?" Carl suggested. "Bailey could climb to the top of the tree and shout something like, 'This is the voice of God and I will strike you down with lightning if you don't let those children go!' "

"And their dogs," Ingrid added.

"Sure!" Bailey whispered. "In what language?"

The others looked so dejected that Bailey took pity on them. "Don't panic!" he whispered. "I'll think of a way. Maybe bug spray would do the trick. Or how about a portable radio? If I turned that up full blast, I bet it would scare the pants off them! I'll go home and get it."

"They aren't wearing pants," said Carl. "Besides, you can't go home. If you climb down to draw a window in the path, they'll tie you up just like us."

Knowing this to be true, Bailey did something that took all the courage he could muster. He shut his eyes and drew an invisible rectangle in the air below his branch. Then he jumped inside.

Instead of landing on the moist, black jungle floor as he had feared, Bailey landed on a mattress. Opening his eyes with a sigh of relief, he leaped off the bed, flung open the door, and stopped dead in his tracks. At the top of the attic stairs, holding a pail of soapy water in one hand and a sponge in the other, stood his aunt.

"Goodness!" she gasped. "You gave me a start! What are you up to? I thought you were all outside."

"We are," Bailey said truthfully. "All except me, that is. What are *you* up to?"

"I thought I'd give that wall of yours a good scrub," said Mrs. Carlson. "The one over your bed. It looks as if someone had been walking all over it with muddy feet."

Bailey shut the door firmly behind him and forced himself to smile. "I like it that way," he told his aunt.

Mrs. Carlson laughed. "That's kind of you, Bailey, but I'm sure you'd like it better clean. Why, if your mother saw it, I'd blush!"

Bailey thought of the window that he had painted on the wall. What if his aunt walked in and saw it? What would she say when she noticed that it was alive? Or worse still, if she could see her children captives of the blue-green tribe? Or worst of all, if she couldn't see the magic and insisted on washing the whole picture—cannibals, children, dogs, and all—off the wall?

Bailey shuddered. "Give me that sponge, Aunt Ellen. I'll do it myself."

Setting down the bucket, Mrs. Carlson stared at Bailey in amazement. "Goodness!" she said. "I can't imagine what's come over you recently, but it's become a real pleasure to have you around!"

"I know," said Bailey coldly. "You mean you didn't want me around before." He picked up the bucket, took the sponge from his aunt's hand, and went back to his room.

The more he thought about it, the more horrified Bailey was by the danger of the situation. The other Vikings and their dogs were probably on the verge of being chopped up for cannibal stew. If he went back to rescue them, by whatever means, his aunt might come and wash the window off the wall. But if he stayed to guard the attic room, who knew what horrible tortures the others would undergo?

Searching desperately for a solution, Bailey took a pencil and doodled on a piece of scratch paper. He drew a picture of his Aunt Ellen with a top hat, vampire teeth, and glasses. He drew a picture of his cousin Carl wearing high heels and a wreath of roses in his hair. Then he forced himself to look back at the window of the south sea island.

The water rippled, the wind blew through the coconana palms, and the beach looked peaceful and inviting. If only they had never left the beach! There were tears in Bailey's eyes as he sketched stick figures of Carl and Anna on the sand. Sadly he added Ingrid and the Viking dogs.

To his astonishment, the figures came to life. Ingrid and his cousins moved slowly, as if their joints were stiff, while the dogs danced around them, wagging their tails.

With a shout of joy, Bailey leaped through the window, drew a rectangle in the sand around the Vikings, and brought them home again.

Anna, Carl, and Ingrid were bewildered. "What happened?" Carl asked. "One minute we were tied to the tree and the next we were back on the beach again!"

"It was about time," Ingrid added. "They had a fire going, and there was water in the pot."

Anna was trembling. "I've had enough magic windows. Each one is scarier than the last!"

"How did you rescue us?" asked Carl.

"It was easy!" said Bailey. "I just drew you in and then I went in to get you."

"But it wasn't the same us!" Anna wailed. "It was *new* us, and the old us are going to be eaten by cannibals!"

The others hardly heard what Anna said, because a thought suddenly occurred to all three of them at once: *Would it work with Fox?*

 "When I wanted a penguin, all Bailey had to do was paint one in Central Park," said Carl.

"And when we wanted free pizza, Bailey just made a sign that said 'Free Pizza,'" Ingrid said.

"That's right!" said Anna, who had finally caught on. "And to rescue us from the cannibals, he drew us on the beach."

Bailey was grinning from ear to ear. "What a dope I was! All I had to do was draw a picture of Fox and then go in and get him. That's what the man with the funny eyes meant when he said to use my brains."

"Well, do it!" said Carl. "Do it now, before it's too late. Remember, the man said your time was running out."

"There's only one problem," said Bailey, and he told the others about Mrs. Carlson wanting to wash the wall. "You can hardly blame her," he added. "It really does look dingy."

The Vikings stared at Bailey's wall. In a few weeks' time,

ten windows had come and gone. One way or another, each had left its mark.

"It's not our fault," Ingrid grumbled. "It's the fault of the person who didn't put a real window over Bailey's bed."

"Never mind about that," said Carl. "Bailey can trade beds with me if he likes. It's the magic that matters. What are you going to paint now, Bailey?"

"Nothing," said Bailey. "Just Fox."

In his left hand, Bailey held the engraving from the church bazaar. In his right hand he held his brush. He had never been much good at drawing dogs, but by copying as closely as possible, he ended up with a likeness of Fox on the bedroom wall. The jester in the background of the engraving seemed to be laughing at Bailey while he worked.

The tension was almost unbearable as the Vikings waited for the black-and-white puppy to come to life. They had almost given up hope when at last his eyes began to glisten and his nose began to shine. Even his fur looked like real fur, instead of the rough strokes made by Bailey's brush.

Fox cocked his head to one side and scratched behind his left ear. Then he stood up and shook himself all over. Staring out of the window at Bailey, he wagged his tail.

"Hurry up!" said Bailey. He had already thrown one leg over the windowsill when Carl caught him by the seat of his pants.

"You fool!" Carl shouted. "Look where you're going!"

Bailey looked and turned pale. On the other side of the window there was nothing to jump down on. It was like looking up into the sky on a clear day. If Bailey had jumped, he would never have stopped falling.

Bailey climbed back into the attic room. "Why isn't Fox falling?" he asked.

"I don't know," said Carl. "But if I were you, I'd put a floor under him, just to make sure."

Bailey was not interested in painting a good place to visit. All he wanted was to bring Fox home, so he simply drew what he had learned in art class at school: perspective. Using Carl's ruler, he made four straight lines leading to a point in the center of the window. When he had finished, it was as if he were looking down a long corridor.

Carl approved. "That's more like it! Now Fox has a floor and walls and a ceiling. He can't get out."

The Vikings decided that only two of them should go to rescue Fox. Carl and Anna would stay home with the dogs in case their mother came to wash the wall while Bailey and Ingrid were on the other side.

"Why can't Eric the Red come, too?" asked Ingrid.

"She might scare Fox away," Carl explained.

"I'm sure they'll be good friends," Bailey added, "but it's kinder to let them take their time getting to know each other."

Even though the dogs stayed home, something frightened Fox when the children stepped through the window. He turned and scampered down the corridor as fast as his puppy legs would go. Bailey ran after him, and Ingrid followed Bailey. Since the walls of the corridor were absolutely blank, they didn't seem to be going anywhere. Even so, Fox got farther and farther ahead of them, until he disappeared. At last Bailey and Ingrid stopped to catch their breath.

"It's no good!" Bailey said bitterly. "The magic is just playing tricks on us again. We'll never get Fox back. Never!"

"Maybe we ought to go home and draw a cage around him," Ingrid suggested. "Then he'd be sure to stay put."

Bailey shook his head. "Something would go wrong. It always does."

Ingrid tried to comfort him, but Bailey didn't hear a word she said. He was so wrapped in his thoughts that he didn't even notice when a dog began to bark.

Ingrid jumped up and looked around. "Hey, Bailey, cheer up!" she shouted. "I hear Fox, and look where we are!"

Instead of the endless corridor of a few moments earlier, the children found themselves in a dusty little room. There were shelves on every wall, from the floor up to the ceiling. Sitting behind a small table was a jester. He wore motley, like the jester in the engraving, and he wore a cap with bells. Since he was in color now, the children noticed that he also had one blue eye and one brown.

"You're late!" he told them severely.

"But we ran as fast as we could!" Ingrid protested.

The jester shook his head. "Oh, no-no-no-no-no!" he scolded them. "Never run in the corridor! You're late, and I won't take any excuses."

It didn't make sense, and Ingrid told him so. "How can you be late when there's nothing to be late for?"

The jester sighed. "You seemed quite intelligent children," he said. "Especially the boy who paints the windows. I expected him to make good use of his magic, but he frittered it away. No brains! Well, never mind. Take your dog and go away. Unless you find something more tempting."

"More tempting!" Ingrid echoed. "What do you mean?"

The man waved toward the shelves on the wall. "Look around you," he said. "Take your time and make your choice. Either the dog or something else, but not both. That's the way the magic works."

The shelves were crowded with fascinating objects, but the first thing the children noticed was Fox. He was sitting on a shelf between a pair of seven-league boots and a bottle marked "Good Luck."

Bailey gathered the puppy into his arms, but Ingrid couldn't help looking at the other items on the shelves. There were not only the presents you would like for Christmas, such as fifty-pound boxes of chocolates and musical roller skates. There were also things you know it would be no use asking for, like wings, and invisibility pills, and stories that never ended.

There were pictures to hang on your wall in which people talked and walked around. There were bags of seeds that would grow into a forest overnight if you thought it might be fun to play in a forest the next day. There were instant playmates: You just added water and they expanded to the proper size. There were potions to swallow that would make you into all sorts of things you had always hoped to be.

Ingrid was not interested in the potions for becoming divinely beautiful or angelically good, but she was fascinated by a bottle that read "Education Solution: Three drops for each year of school."

Ingrid was in fifth grade and thought school a terrible waste of time. She had often calculated the number of years before she finished her education: seven at the very least and eleven if she went to college. How convenient if she could do it all with one gulp! Even the most horrid-tasting medicine would be worthwhile.

It was impossible to resist. Turning her back to Bailey, Ingrid pulled out the cork and drank.

Bailey's reunion with Fox was wet and noisy. Wet because Fox licked Bailey on the nose and behind the ears. Noisy because Bailey laughed and Fox barked and they both jumped up and down.

Once these formalities were over, Bailey looked for Ingrid, but she had disappeared. In her place was a tall young woman with a conceited face.

"Excuse me," said Bailey. "Do you know where my friend went?"

The young woman smiled at him condescendingly. "I know everything," she said.

For a moment, Bailey forgot that he was looking for Ingrid. He had always wanted to meet someone who knew everything. He had even prepared a list of questions in case he did.

"Is there life on other planets?" he demanded, his eyes gleaming.

"That depends on your definition of *life*," said the young woman.

Knowing that it was no use trying to define life, Bailey asked another question. "Who will be the next president of the United States?"

The young woman looked annoyed. "I never discuss politics with children!" she snapped.

"Well, then," said Bailey, "can you tell me where Fox came from and who his parents were?"

"What utter nonsense!" the young woman sputtered. "Who could possibly care?"

"*I* care," said Bailey. "Can you at least tell me what I'm going to get for Christmas?"

"Don't be ridiculous!" said the young woman. "You can't expect me to squander a college education on trivia like that."

"Oh, never mind," said Bailey. "Just tell me where Ingrid is."

"Ingrid?" repeated the young woman, with her eyebrows raised in amusement. "Why, my name is Ingrid, and I'm right here!"

Bailey stared at her and began to wonder. He recognized the skinny brown pigtails and the big blue eyes. The woman was wearing clothes like Ingrid's, too, only they were so tight that they were splitting at the seams. He looked suspiciously at the empty bottle in her hand. After reading the label, he understood.

"Aw, Ingrid!" he wailed. "You jerk! What a dumb thing to do!"

Ingrid looked at the bottle, too, but didn't seem to recognize it. "What are you talking about?" she asked.

"You went and chose something without asking me!" Bailey said angrily. "Now we can't have Fox, and just look at you!"

Ingrid fluffed up her hair and smoothed down her T-shirt. "I'm a mess!" she said in the complacent voice some women use when they secretly think they look quite nice.

"You sure are," said Bailey. "You look awful! What do you think your grandmother is going to say when you get back?"

"When I get back where?" Ingrid asked.

"Back home, of course," said Bailey.

Ingrid smiled. "You're sweet," she told Bailey, "but I'm rather busy just now, so why don't you run along?"

Her honeyed voice made Bailey feel sick. He hated grown-ups who changed their voices when they talked to children. At last he lost his temper.

"You cheated!" he shouted. "You ruined everything! I'm going to leave you here and take Fox anyway!"

He turned and started running towards the door only to find that there was no longer any door.

The jester chuckled. "Only one goody to share between you," he reminded Bailey. "Unless the young lady wants to change her mind."

Bailey knew trying to get Ingrid to change her mind was useless because she couldn't remember what her mind had been like before. She hadn't recognized Bailey and didn't even notice Fox. Bailey thought she was dreadful since she had swallowed the Education Solution, but he hated to go home without her.

"Don't you want to see Anna again?" he asked. "Don't you care about the Vikings?"

Ingrid's eyes were blank. "Vikings?" she repeated. "I don't know what you're talking about."

Bailey hugged Fox tight to keep from crying. "I liked you better the way you were!" he told her.

He wished he could shut out Ingrid's shrill titter and the jester's chuckle. The chuckle grew louder and louder until it turned into a harsh, unfriendly bark.

"Stop laughing!" Bailey shouted. "Can't you hear me? Stop laughing!"

All at once he realized that it wasn't laughter after all. It was a real bark, coming from far away up the endless corridor, outside the dusty room. What's more, the door to the corridor was back where it belonged, and it was open.

Ingrid's face lit up. "Eric," she whispered. Then she shouted, "Eric the Red! Let me out of here!"

Bailey gave a sigh of relief as he watched her shrink into her normal size. "Whew!"

"Whew what?" asked Ingrid in her normal voice. "Have you got Fox? Because I think it's time we went home."

The jester shook his head regretfully. "What a waste of magic," he said. "No brains! No brains! Think of all the things you might have done. The whole world was open to you!"

"I don't want the whole world," said Bailey. "All I want is Fox."

Still hugging his dog, he grabbed Ingrid's hand and pulled her out of the room.

Carl and Anna were wild with excitement at the sight of Fox. Even the Viking dogs, after some preliminary circling and sniffing, gave their seal of approval by wagging their tails.

There was such joy in the attic room that Mr. and Mrs. Carlson ran upstairs to see what was causing the commotion. When they saw the new dog and Bailey's latest window, their faces showed a mixture of bewilderment and disapproval.

"Who's *that* fellow?" asked Mr. Carlson, pointing at Fox. "I never saw him before—is he a stray?"

"That's no stray!" Bailey said indignantly. "He's mine. His name is Fox."

Carl knew that if Bailey said any more, he would give away their secret. He made up a story quickly. "He's—uh—been around quite a lot lately," he told his father. "I'm pretty sure he doesn't have an owner. Other than Bailey, I mean. It's okay if Bailey keeps him, isn't it?"

Mr. Carlson looked doubtful. "That depends on Bailey's parents. Besides, someone is bound to claim him one of these days. Doesn't he have any tags? I suppose not, if Bailey named him after his friend Fox."

Meanwhile, Mrs. Carlson was staring at the wall. "Why, Bailey!" she cried. "That wall doesn't look one bit cleaner than before. And what's that strange design you've been painting on it?"

"Sorry, Aunt Ellen," said Bailey. "I'll wash it now, I promise."

Mr. Carlson walked over and inspected the wall more closely. "I wouldn't bother to wash it," he said. "What this whole room needs is a new coat of paint. We can do it next week, after Bailey leaves."

"After Bailey leaves!" Ingrid wailed. "Are you sending him away? What for?"

"You're leaving, too, honey," Mrs. Carlson reminded her. "Tomorrow is Labor Day, and Tuesday is the first day of school."

 Ingrid woke up the next morning with a heavy, sad feeling in her throat. It took a moment to remember why. When she remembered, she rolled over and buried her face in the pillow.

"I have to go home!" she moaned. "And Bailey does, too."

Summer was over. It seemed unfair that the fields and trees would be there all the same outside her window, even after she was gone.

"Are you awake, Ingrid?" her grandmother called. "Time to get up and finish packing. You're missing a beautiful morning!"

Ingrid sat up and opened her eyes. It was an autumn sort of day. The sun was shining but it was fragile sunlight, and the air was crisp and cool. Hearing familiar voices, Ingrid ran to the window and looked out. There were Bailey, Carl, and Anna, talking to her grandmother on the front walk.

"You picked a good day to visit!" Mrs. Werbeski told them cheerfully. "Bossy had her calf last night! Ronald is in the barn with her now. And when you're through looking, come back to the kitchen. Ingrid hasn't had her breakfast yet, and I'm sure you won't refuse a bit more yourselves."

Ingrid dressed quickly and ran to join her friends in the barn. "Congratulations, Bossy!" she said. "Many happy returns of the day! Congratulations, Uncle Ronald!"

Ronald Werbeski chuckled. "I'm not the father, Ingrid. I'm just a friend."

The new calf was a soft beige color with big brown eyes, almost more like a deer than a cow.

"What are you going to name him?" Anna asked.

"It's a heifer," said Ronald Werbeski. "We haven't thought of a name for her yet. Got any ideas?"

"How about 'Meek'?" Carl suggested. "Because meek is the opposite of bossy."

"But she's just *like* Bossy!" Ingrid objected.

Anna reached over and stroked the calf's rough, warm fur. "Why not 'Bambi,' because she's like a deer?"

"Bambi was a boy," said Bailey. "She ought to have a girl's name. What's Mrs. Werbeski's name?"

"Ruby," said Ronald.

"That's a nice name," said Bailey. "Why don't you call the calf 'Ruby Werbeski'?"

When she was told at breakfast, Ingrid's grandmother said that she was tickled pink. " 'Ruby Werbeski'!" she kept repeating. "Glory be! What a name for a heifer!"

"It's a good name," Anna assured her. "We can call her 'Ruby' for short. It was Bailey's idea."

"Well, what do you know about that!" said Mrs. Werbeski. "Whatever will you think of next, Bailey Bond?"

"Nothing," Bailey said dully, "because I'm not going to be here. This afternoon I have to go home."

Mrs. Werbeski pulled a sheet of biscuits from the oven. She opened the refrigerator and took out a pitcher of cold milk.

"Ingrid told me," she said. "Fact is, it's going to be lonesome without you two around."

"Bailey will come back next summer," said Anna with her mouth full of buttered biscuit. "We want him to come back every summer and maybe Christmas, too."

"Is that so?" said Mrs. Werbeski. "You've changed your tune since the day he came, haven't you!"

Ingrid blushed and took a big gulp of milk.

"Well, I'll be sorry to see you leave," Mrs. Werbeski told Bailey. "Though goodness knows, I wouldn't have said it a month ago."

The Carlson children couldn't bear to talk about it anymore. They stood up and wiped the white moustaches from their upper lips. They thanked Mrs. Werbeski for breakfast. They said good-bye to Ingrid and promised to write to her in Chicago.

Carl, Anna, and Bailey slouched as they shuffled along the road, kicking up clouds of dust. No one felt like making conversation. Even Leif the Lucky looked a little down at the mouth.

They were halfway home when they heard Ronald Werbeski shouting behind them. His face was red from running hard, but he grinned. "Forgot to give you this for your mother!" he panted, handing a light blue envelope to Anna. "It got delivered to our house by mistake, a while back."

"It must be from Aunt Frannie," Anna told Bailey as she slipped it into her pocket. "She always writes on light blue paper."

Bailey wasn't interested. "It can't be very important, because I'm seeing her tonight."

Instead of turning up the Carlsons' driveway, which was the short way home, the children followed a path that twisted through the woods. After a quarter of a mile, the path crossed a clearing full of milkweed pods. If you looked up close, you saw that some of the pods weren't really pods at all.

"They're monarch butterfly cocoons!" said Bailey, touching one gently. "I wish I could take one back to the city and watch it hatch."

"Go right ahead!" Carl said generously. "We've got more than we need."

But Bailey shook his head. "He wouldn't find the right things to eat when he came out of his cocoon. He'd be unhappy."

"I guess I'm like butterflies," said Anna. "I'd be simply furious if I went to sleep in the country and woke up in the city."

"Think of me tomorrow morning," said Bailey gloomily. "Fox will hate it, too. The city is no place to raise a dog. You two are lucky that you get to live here all year round."

Anna forgot about the letter until lunchtime. "This went to the Werbeskis by mistake," she told her mother as she fished it out of her pocket.

Mrs. Carlson stopped eating to open the letter. "For goodness' sake!" she exclaimed. "This was sent ages ago! How long did the Werbeskis have it, Anna? Why, to think we might not have read this until after Bailey left for the airport!"

"What does it say?" asked Anna.

"Bailey is going to California after all," said Mrs. Carlson. "His parents like it so much out there that they're going to stay all winter. Your Uncle Jed found a job, and they even have a school lined up for Bailey."

No one who saw Bailey's face would have thought this was good news. He looked more as if it were a catastrophe. "But if I live in California, I can't come here for Christmas!" he wailed.

Mrs. Carlson laughed. "Were you planning on coming for Christmas?"

"We invited him," said Anna. "We invited him for Thanksgiving and Easter and Mother's Day, too."

"That would have been nice," said Mrs. Carlson, "but I'm sure Bailey will like California."

"Fox won't like it, that's for sure," said Bailey.

His uncle smiled. "I wouldn't count on taking Fox to California, Bailey. I'm afraid we'll have to make some attempt to find his owner."

It did no good for Carl to kick Bailey under the table. Bailey's face was already changing back to the way it had looked when he first arrived.

"*I'm* his owner!" he said stubbornly. "I told you that before. If you don't believe me, ask my mother. And if Fox can't come to California, I'm not going, either."

Anna changed the subject quickly. "Is Bailey flying to New York City today, or is he going straight out west?" she asked her mother.

"Neither," said Mrs. Carlson. "That's what I was about to tell you. Aunt Frannie is flying back to sublet the apartment and pack up a few things, and then she's driving up here to get Bailey herself. They won't be leaving for Los Angeles until the tenth."

"Hurray! That means Bailey can stay one more week!" shouted Anna.

Bailey remembered another "Hurray!" that Anna had shouted a month before, over the telephone. He grinned and winked at Anna. "One more week?" he repeated. "Just think of all the places we can go!"

"Don't forget, Carl and Anna will be in school, even if you aren't," Mr. Carlson warned Bailey. "Since you're sticking around, you might give me a hand painting the attic room."

Bailey and his uncle painted the room a pale shade of yellow. It looked more cheerful, especially after the crisp, clear autumn weather turned to rain. Four days later, when they had just finished and were upstairs admiring their handiwork, they heard a car pull up the driveway.

"It's your mother!" Mr. Carlson told Bailey, leaning out the open window. "I hope she's not afraid of dogs—she's getting quite a welcome!"

Bailey leaned out, too, and saw Fox and Leif the Lucky leaping enthusiastically at his mother with muddy paws. "Hi, Mom!" he shouted. "Don't worry, they're just being friendly."

His mother looked up and waved. "It's okay. I'm in jeans. How on earth did Fox get here, Bailey? Or am I seeing things?"

Mr. Carlson looked puzzled. "Are you trying to tell me you recognize that stray?" he called. "That's incredible!"

During the next few days, the children put all their energy into avoiding questions about Fox. The Carlson parents and Bailey's mother couldn't get over the fact that he had been lost in New York City and found in upper New York State. They felt it was too good a story not to be shared, and they wanted to send it to the papers. But the children were wary of publicity. What if they were photographed and someone recognized them as the children in pajamas who had accompanied a talking penguin to the Central Park Zoo?

Meanwhile, Bailey was happier than he had ever hoped to be. Not only had his mother been willing to bring Fox to California, but also she had informed Bailey, to his surprise, that their new house was not in Los Angeles but in the country, forty miles away. Best of all, she had said that Bailey could accept the Carlsons' invitation to come the next year not just for the month of August, but for the entire summer.

On the ninth of September, the day before he was to leave with his mother for California, Bailey crept up to the attic room while his cousins were in school. On the newly painted wall, very lightly but precisely, he drew a window of the Yankee Stadium. Not that he intended to go inside; he was too afraid of meeting the jester. But he wanted to see if he and the other Vikings could continue their adventures the following year.

He sat watching for an hour, but the window never came to life. At last he took a sponge and washed it all away.

"If it makes you feel any better," he told his cousins that night, "we couldn't go through another window even if I stayed. I tried, and the magic is gone."

Anna was surprised. "Do you think that's because you and Daddy painted the wall? Maybe the magic was in the first coat of paint!"

"Who knows?" said Bailey. "Something else is different, too. Look at the engraving of the puppy!"

Anna looked and gasped. "The jester isn't there anymore! I

wonder what that means. Do you think the engraving was magic, too?"

"If it was, it isn't now," said Bailey. "It looks just the same as when you bought it at the bazaar, and that's fine with me."

"Where did the magic go?" asked Anna.

"It probably moved to somebody else's wall," said Bailey. "When it gets tired of living in one place, it picks up and moves to another."

"Here today, gone tomorrow!" said Carl.

"Except that it's gone today, so maybe it will be *back* tomorrow," Anna said hopefully.

Tomorrow came, but the only unusual event was the arrival in the mail of a package for Bailey Bond. Inside was a chemistry set, only slightly used, accompanied by a note that said:

USE YOUR BRAINS!